DOUBLE FEATURE
Gemini Error/Chrome Justice

Anthony D. Phillips Jr.

DREAMERPUBLISHING

Cleveland, Ohio

DEDICATION

This book is dedicated to all of the readers that have supported my endeavors over the years. Thank you from the bottom of my heart. The support is greatly appreciated.

CONTENTS

ACKNOWLEDGMENTS

First, I would like to say thank you to all of the people that supported me and spoke blessings of prosperity into my life. It is because of you, that I decided to revise these short tales. Enjoy. (P.S. Chrome Justice comic book series coming soon)

Gemini Error

PRELUDE
INTRODUCTION TO ERROR

INSIDE the home of Mr. and Mrs. Struthers, an intense argument is ensuing. Mrs. Struthers has just arrived home after staying out all night with her friends. The tension in the air is at suffocating levels.

"I told you I had a girl's night out with Trisha and Alicia! I got too drunk, and I ended up sleeping in Alicia's guest room. That's all, I promise you!" Amanda protests as her husband hurls accusations at her. She has a pounding headache from the night before, and her outer appearance clearly shows evidence of a night of debauchery. Her long, jet-black hair is tangled and matted with a mixture of hair products, sweat, and naturally produced oils, red faded, smeared lipstick covers her soft pouty lips. Her light brown skin is sticky with old sweat. The cheeks on her face have a slight tinge of red. The smell of alcohol is still detectable on her breath. Her tight exposing dress, is something that a married woman has no business even thinking about purchasing, let alone wearing.

"Look, I know something's going on so don't try to make me think otherwise! That's like saying shit don't stink!" Mr. Struthers yells furiously as spittle shoots out of his now foaming mouth. He knows that something isn't right. He smells the faint scent of cologne mixed in with the overbearing stench of alcohol on her. His disheveled appearance, his brown thinning mess of hair is wildly unattractive; he reeks of cigarettes, weed, and days of not bathing. His dingy wife beater hangs and is slightly stretched out from repeated wear. "Oh, and I guess Alicia sprays her guest room bedding with cologne huh?" Even through his smoke scent filled nostrils, he knows when he smells a masculine scent.

"See there you go with that shit again! You're always getting so mad and riled up over nothing! You need anger management! I hate when you get that crazy look in your eyes and start foaming at the mouth!"

"Oh so now I need anger management cause my wife's out fucking some joker behind my back! Mandy I know something ain't right, your friends can't cover for you forever!"

"I told you that I don't like being called Mandy it sounds too white, and if you want to believe that you're married to a hoe, then you might as well not be with me! I told you it wasn't going to happen again! I make one little mistake and I end up paying for it for the rest of my life! You had a choice to leave or forgive me and work it out! You chose to work it out! What you need to do is get over your insecurity trip cause I'm not the problem!" With that said Amanda leaves the room. Carl contemplates following her and continuing until he feels satisfied, but after staying up practically the whole night, he doesn't have the strength. He just lets it go. "I guess I shouldn't have dated outside of my race." He mumbles as he thinks back to one of the last conversations that he had with his old man before they fell out. He remembers his father telling him that he would no longer be a part of the family if he chose to be with Amanda Perez. He can just hear his father saying, "I told you so".

In another part of the house, Amanda's guilt is getting the best of her.

She doesn't have the heart to tell Carl the truth. She knows that it will hurt him even more than the first time. She wonders if she should simply file for divorce and spare his already broken pride and shattered feelings. From a legal standpoint, it would be in her best interest not to tell him. She could request a divorce due to negligence of husbandly duties, which wouldn't be that far from the truth. As of late, Carl hasn't been the best husband. His depression has caused him to be withdrawn and combative. His lack of financial stability and the fact he has quite gotten over Amanda's first affair has caused him to become highly insecure. Even before she crossed the line and strayed outside of the marriage for the second time, he was already accusing her of cheating especially after he became laid-off. In some weird twisted way, his accusations pushed her away and into the arms of another man. She knows that he really doesn't deserve what she's doing to him. He deserves so much better. Amanda goes into the bathroom, locks the door, falls to her knees, and starts to sob uncontrollably. It is definitely not, the way that she intended to spend the morning after a great night.

Meanwhile, inside the office of Attorney Arnold Spellman, Private Investigator Malcolm Scott sits with the attorney as he discusses his current case. Arnold Spellman has features that are very Morris Chestnut-esque. His dark smooth creaseless skin, tender eyes, handsome smile, and stature, make many women long to be Mrs. Spellman. Arnold Spellman is one of the highest regarded black attorneys in the city, and even though he hates the label "One of the city's best black attorneys", he accepts the acknowledgement never the less. He hates living in a world that is so fixated on class and color, mainly the latter. No matter how much he excels, or how many honors he achieves, his color is always the first thing that most notice.

"Mr. Scott I need you to gather as much evidence as possible on the extramarital activities of my client's husband Harold Atkins." Mr. Spellman says as he lays a yellow envelope on the desk in front of him. "I need to build a strong enough case against the guy. I want it to be so solid that the judge doesn't even want to hear two words from him. I need concrete, irrefutable proof and I need it within a timely manner. How soon can you have it ready?" Mr. Spellman expresses while maintaining eye contact with the bleach blond, blue-eyed detective. Malcolm Scott is a person that people often describe as someone that doesn't live up to his full potential. With his handsome boyish looks, he could've easily been a heartthrob having his fair share of women, but he chose to pursue his childhood dream instead. He was always a big crime show buff. As a child, he would watch reruns of "Magnum P.I.", "Remington Steele", and "Murder she wrote". Even with the few extra pounds that he's managed to put on over the years, he is still a rather attractive specimen.

"Uh give me a few days and let me see what I can put together. I should have all of the evidence you need within a week's time." Malcolm responds as he opens up the yellow envelope and looks through its contents. He takes out a picture of Harold. While Malcolm studies the picture, Attorney Spellman takes out his checkbook. He writes out a check, detaches it from the book, and gives it to him. Malcolm briefly diverts his attention away from the picture and focuses it on the check. Satisfied with the amount written on it he smiles and neatly tucks it into the pocket of his suit coat. "I will contact you by the end of this week and let you know what I have." Malcolm says before leaving the attorney's office with the check and yellow envelope in hand. As he

4

walks down the hall, Malcolm continues to stare at the picture. He hates men like Harold. He believes men like Harold make it hard for good guys. They are also the reason why Malcolm loves his job. He loves helping expose two timing losers. After P.I. Scott leaves, Attorney Spellman places a call to Harold's wife Denise Atkins.

"Hello Denise. This is Attorney Spellman. I was calling to inform you that I've found a way to get the evidence we need against your husband, but I'm going to need you to help me out."

"Okay sure what else do you need?"

"Well for starters I'm going to need access to your husband's cell phone account and I'm also going to need you to enable the GPS tracking function on his phone. It would also be helpful if you gave us a list of his friends and acquaintances."

"Alright, it might take a few days, but I'm sure that I can get all of that handled. So once it's all done, how long do you think it will take to get some substantial evidence?"

"Um it should take no more than two weeks tops to compile enough evidence to get the ball rolling. I already have someone working on it as we speak. He's a real straight shooter so I know he will get us exactly what we need. Trust me we're going to get you everything that you deserve Mrs. Atkins."

"Thank you Mr. Spellman."

"You're welcome. I will be in touch" Attorney Spellman finishes the conversation and quickly dials up P. I. Scott. Mr. Scott is in the middle of eating when he picks up the phone.

"Hey Mr. Spellman, what can I help you with?" He asks in a garbled tone in between bites of food.

"Hey Malcolm, I have some more things that might make your job

5

easier…"

DAY 1

12:05pm: Amanda pulls up to Harold's company. As she exits her vehicle, Harold greets her. Harold fits the tall dark and handsome label to a tee. His olive toned skin, dark hair with slight sprinkles of gray, chiseled facial features, cool grayish blue eyes, and muscular toned frame, make it hard for the opposite sex to shy away from him. Harold places a quick peck on her cheek as they embrace. They then get in her car and proceed to their destination.

"I had a great time the other night," Amanda says while keeping her eyes focused on the road.

"I did too. I'm glad that I was able to get you for a whole night. It was awesome!" Harold responds as he reminisces.

"So be honest, do you have anyone else?" Amanda asks and hopes that Harold responds exactly how she envisions in her head.

"Does it matter? I mean you're still married and you obliviously know that I'm married... so at the moment exclusivity isn't an option." Harold's answer is bitter but true. It has definitely burst Amanda's bubble, but if she wants to be with him, she has no choice but to accept it.

12:18pm: The couple arrives at one of Harold's favorite restaurants, "Toni's". "Toni's" is an upscale eatery on the eastside of town. The city's social elite frequent it. Its exclusivity is what keeps them coming back. Lost in a moment of passion, Harold places an intimate kiss on Amanda's lips before they exit the vehicle. Unbeknownst to Harold, every detail of the kiss; is being recorded. Malcolm has been following them since they left Harold's office. Harold and Amanda exit her vehicle. Preoccupied with the lust and excitement of the moment, both are oblivious to everything else around them. Malcolm watches them walk into the restaurant holding hands. He snaps a quick series of photos. He makes sure to get as many pictures within those few seconds as possible. He wants to follow them inside and get juicier footage, but he knows that it would go against his rule of never getting physically too close to the subject. Malcolm resists his urge and stays in the car to avoid detection.

Once inside the restaurant, an atmosphere of class surrounds Harold and Amanda. The walls of the restaurant are a deep wine color with subtle dark chocolate wood accents. The lighting is flawlessly set to suit the relaxed contemporary environment. Plush private booths line the walls. Circular shaped glass tables, trimmed with classy dark polished wood, occupy the space in the main dining area. As surprising as it is, this is Amanda's first time visiting "Toni's". She takes it all in as they approach the host of the restaurant. The host is a husky mulatto man named James. James has seen Harold come in on so many different occasions in the company of so many different women that it sickens him. He sees the light brown Latina beauty and envy instantly sets in. Her long dark hair perfectly accentuates her facial features. Her slim but curvy frame screams for attention. James can't stand Harold. If it were not for the fact that Harold is good friends with the restaurant's owner, James would have done everything in his power to expose him ages ago. Deep down, James despises guys like Harold. He feels that it's people like Harold that get everything in life (including an abundance of women), and leaves scraps and broken hearts for men like himself to deal with. James has memorized Harold's favorite dishes. Every time he orders any of them, James makes sure to add a little something extra to them as his way of winning one for the "little guys".

"Hello, welcome to Toni's, my name is James, how may I help you today?" James hates having to force himself to say that line every time Harold visits with a new piece of meat on his arm. He hates it but does it for the sake of keeping his job and receiving a more than generous tip at the end of each visit. Harold is everything that James is not, handsome, charming, rich, and successful.

"Hello James, my name is Harold Atkins and I have a reservation for two." Harold responds with a smug pearly white smile. He releases his lines so well, that he could've easily been an A list actor, effortlessly going toe to toe with the likes of Brad Pit,

Tom Cruise, and Denzel Washington. He is as slick as snot! James opens the reservation book and pretends to thumb through it.

"Alright Mr. Atkins, I see your name. If you would be so kind as to follow me, I will show you and your guest to your seats." James retorts as he flashes a fake smile. He knows exactly where to seat them. Harold always calls thirty to forty-five minutes before hand to make sure his same section will be ready for him. He always sits in the private area divided from the rest of the restaurant and devoid of windows. This is how he has kept the same game working since forever. Harold and Amanda take their seats. The passion between them is as hot as ever. Amanda knows that what they're doing is wrong but she feels so alive when she is in his presence. He makes her feel something that she hasn't felt in years. Something that Carl has failed to produce.

"So what made you want me back? I thought you were trying to work it out with your husband?" Harold asks as he studies Amanda. She is even more beautiful than he remembers. He knows that he's dead wrong. He knows the consequences of messing with a married woman. He remembers what happened with their last go round, all of the drama and unneeded stress, but their tawdry affair is like a drug. It gives him a rush unlike any other thing that he has experienced. The thrill of messing with a married woman is unrivaled. It is a burning desire, one that can only be satisfied with the right element.

"I couldn't stay away… I tried to make it work but…we're just too far-gone. It's dead. Our relationship is over. Carl still wants to hang on but it's useless. He's stuck on weed again and chain smoking those disgusting cigarettes! Plus, he's still out of work and on unemployment." Amanda feels terrible, speaking so unfavorably about her husband, but she has to vent to someone. It is just too much to keep bottled up to herself. She has tried to tell her friends Trisha and Alicia. They have already told her that she was stupid for going back in the first place. The only thing that they are useful for is providing an alibi. "Harold I'm ready for you. I'm ready for us." Amanda places her hand on Harold's hand. They look into each other's eyes and share a deep intimate moment of reflection. Harold really enjoys her company. His feelings for Amanda are deeper than any that he has had for any other woman. He would have already devoted his all to her without second thought, if they were together under less scandalous circumstances. His success is what keeps him trapped in his marriage. All of the money that he potentially would lose to divorce hangs over his head like a cloud full of rain. Getting a divorce would be a sticky, costly situation, one that would surely drain at least half of his assets and net worth. The saying, "It's cheaper to keep her", has never rung so true.

Within minutes of their conversation, a waiter arrives to take their order. Harold, such a creature of habit orders one of his usual dishes and Amanda orders a fresh salad. With everything that she's going through, she doesn't have the appetite to stomach a full lunch.

1:04pm: The happy couple leaves the restaurant hand in hand with bright smiles on their faces. Malcolm snaps more pictures as they enter the vehicle. The car slowly pulls off. Malcolm starts up his vehicle and follows cautiously behind them, maintaining a three-car distance at all times.

1:18pm: The couple arrives back at Harold's company. After a few moments of kissing and fondling, Harold exits the vehicle and goes back to work. From the time they parked, up to the time Harold went back into work, Malcolm has been filming. Harold's days of being a two timing cheat are numbered and he is completely oblivious to it.

2:30pm: Harold receives a call from an unknown woman.

"Hi baby whatcha doing?" A sweet sultry voice inquires on the other end of the line.

"Nothing, just thinking about you my love" is Harold's response.

"Real smooth Mr. Charm the girls' panties off." She responds. "You know I've been missing you sexy. I need to see you." She gushes as Harold smiles in approval of what he is hearing. He loves when he gets them to that point. It's only been a couple of days and she's already having withdrawal.

"So what kind of panties do you have on?" Harold boldly inquires as he leans back in his plush, ultra comfortable leather office chair.

"I have on the kind that was made for you to take off." She responds in an equally bold manner.

"That's what I like to hear. So are we still on for tomorrow?"

"Hell yeah baby, ain't nothing stopping that!" A knock on Harold's office door interrupts his phone conversation

"Come in," he says aloud. "Hey baby, let me call you back a little later. I've got some business to handle."

"Okay don't forget,"

"I won't. I promise." Harold hangs up the phone just as his voluptuous secretary enters the room. Despite her cute face, tantalizing curvaceous frame, and soft smooth medium brown skin, she is probably one of the only women in his life that he has not slept with. The sole reason for this is that he refuses to mix business with pleasure.

"Hello Mr. Atkins, an urgent package just arrived for you," the secretary says as she places a medium sized envelope on his desk.

"Okay. Thanks Michelle." He responds before picking it up. After Michelle leaves, he opens the envelope. He pulls out a handwritten letter. As he reads the letter, the look on his face sours. The lipstick imprint at the bottom of the letter only makes it worse. In a fit of anger, Harold rips and crumbles the letter.

4:02pm: Harold makes a call to his wife. While the phone is ringing, he is entertaining lustful thoughts of Amanda. His thoughts abruptly come to a screeching halt at the sound of his daughter's sweet innocent voice.

"Hello?"

"Hey Janice honey its dad. Let me speak to your mom." He says in the same soft voice he always uses when talking to his precious angel.

"Okay Dad. I love you, hold on." Janice says before putting down the phone. He can hear her calling for Denise as he waits patiently on the phone. Her footfalls echo loudly as she runs to get her mom. Thoughts of Amanda still stalk his conscious. The way her soft skin feels when pressed against his, the taste of her hard erect nipples, the sound of her climax; he almost gets erect just thinking about it.

"Hello," Denise's voice draws his attention back to the phone.

"Hey honey, I was just calling to say I miss you and I will probably be in late. The—" Before Harold can finish his statement, Denise interjects.

"Are you serious? What is it this time, work, your friends, or is it something else? I'm really getting sick of this! You would think that a person of your stature, a successful business owner, would have time for his family!"

"Hold on baby, you really need to take it down a notch. I told you that with the company expansions coming into play that I was going to be putting more hours in at the office. Besides, I don't even go out with my friends that often. On average, I go out with them like what, once every two to three weeks?" Harold clearly presents his case while managing to keep a cool head and maintain a pleasant tone. He has done this so many times that he has mastered the art of diffusing a potentially dramatic situation.

"Well…"

"Exactly, so let's not cause any discord in our relationship. I love you and I think about you all the time. Everything that I'm doing is for us but anyway, I set up something special for Saturday. So when you talk to Britney make sure to tell her that she's on sitter duty for that evening. It will be just us, no Janice, no Britney, no work, and none of my Buddies, just us." Harold knows that mentioning a date for Saturday is all that he needs to do to appease her. He's mastered the art of managing her emotions.

"Um okay." is the only thing that Denise can manage to utter. She wants to be angry with him. She wants to continue giving him a piece of her mind, but a great stillness from within starts to manifest. "I love you too Harold." She says in a low bashful tone. She cannot believe herself. She is ashamed of the way that she lets him gain control over her. She feels weak and in some weird way dependant on his influence over her life. She starts to doubt her gut feelings of Harold's infidelity. She desperately wants to believe in his innocence. She wants to believe his explanations and lies. She wants to believe him but at the same time, she feels like it would be foolish to do so. She contemplates whether she should proceed with the attorney. *"What if I'm being paranoid?"* She thinks to herself as she glances over at her precious angel coloring with her custom art set. The art set is rather expensive for a five year old, but Harold only wants the best for his daughters. He has done very well by them. He has provided them with a life that most, only dream of living.

"Oh yeah, and tell Britney that I'll be able to pick her up from Stacy's house around eight okay? Oh and one more thing, remember that lingerie set that I bought you for Valentine's Day?"

"Yes, the black and silver bustier."

"Yup, that's the one. How about you wear that for me tonight, I feel like doing something special!" Harold says in an exquisitely smooth voice, a voice that makes Denise melt every time she hears it. She feels so foolish but at the same time, so in love. "Honey doll, are you still there?"

"Yes baby, I was just reminiscing about last Valentine's Day." She murmurs as she tries to shake her feelings of doubt.

"Good. Well I'm about to get back to work. I will call you when I'm on my way home."

"Okay," she hangs up the phone and reflects more on her situation.

5:04pm: Harold leaves and goes to the car garage. He checks over his shoulder before getting into one of his favorite cars, a cranberry colored BMW 5 series. Once inside, he sprays himself with his own self-mixed cologne. It is a combination of pricy oils and wintergreen alcohol. He uses it because he hates to smell like another man. He loves individuality. It is something that he swears by.

5:17pm: Harold stops at a Wal-Mart Supercenter. Malcolm

inconspicuously parks and waits a few seconds before following him in. Within minutes of being in the store, Malcolm catches Harold flirting with a woman in produce. After a few minutes of conversation, they exchange numbers.

5:26pm: Harold leaves the store with several incriminating items; condoms, a can of whipped cream, and rose petals, as well as an "All Boys" DVD/CD combo pack. Malcolm manages to get everything on film. He is such a pro at what he does. He gets such a rush from doing things right. As Harold is walking to his car, he notices Malcolm. He pauses for a moment as he stares at the man. Malcolm tenses up slightly but is able to maintain his composure. He looks away and acts as if he is checking a text message on his phone. Harold stops glancing and resumes his walk back to his car.

5:48pm: Harold arrives at a moderately classy hotel on the outskirts of town. Malcolm, always three cars length behind pulls into the parking lot subsequently thereafter. Harold gets out of his car and dials up a number on his cell phone. His smooth walk is uninterrupted by his interaction with the phone.

"I'm here," he says in a crisp effectively smooth voice as he walks through the automatic double doors of the hotel. Once inside, Harold goes to the front desk and starts talking to the attendant. With courteous smiles exchanged, the attendant hands him a keycard. Harold walks from the desk, and continues towards the elevators.

Harold arrives at his destination. He steps out of the elevator on the fifth floor and walks a little ways down the hall before stopping in front of one of the doors. He gently swipes the key card through the slot and the green light flashes accompanied by a soft beep. Upon entering the room, the atmosphere arouses his senses. The glow from lit candles, attract his eyes, soft music playing in the background captivates his ears, and a sweet womanly fragrance seeps into his nostrils. He hears soft splashing coming from the bathroom. Based on the sounds, he assumes that his fantasy is getting ready for a session of ecstasy. He sets down his things and grabs the rose pedals out of the bag. He scatters a few over the bed and proceeds to the bathroom. He gently opens the door and his eyes immediately take in the full naked beauty of Amanda. She smiles affectionately at Harold as she gracefully rinses off the bubbles from her bath. Like performing a scene from a movie, Harold begins placing rose petals on the floor before his naked glistening Puerto Rican beauty. He magically creates a path leading from the tub and ending at the bed. Amanda's eyes light up at the sight of the path. She has a notion to come out of the bathroom naked but decides to stick with her game plan. She dries herself off and grabs the Victoria's Secret bag from off of the bathroom counter. She pulls out the contents of the bag and giddily puts them on.

Harold is getting himself ready for the moment as well. He has been anxious to get another crack at Amanda since the night after the club when she was out with her friends. Amanda emerges from the bathroom in a sheer black mesh and shimmering silver eyelet bustier. Harold's excitement level instantly rises at the sight of her scantily clad curvaceous figure.

"Come and get it Daddy!" She seductively says as she gives Harold her best cum hither look. He mentally salivates at the thought of satisfying his sexual appetite. Harold obeys like a good soldier. Their lips meet in an explosion of passion. They are unable to contain their burning desire. Amanda hops onto Harold and he carries her to the rose pedal covered bed. He places her down and begins attacking her body with a barrage of soft wet kisses. He carefully removes the bustier with a surgeon's precision. Amanda moans in anticipation. She can hardly wait to feel him back inside of her. Each kiss brings her closer to the point of no return. She can no longer wait. She wants his hard strong manhood inside of her. Harold pauses the foreplay session and grabs the whipped cream and condoms. He smiles at Amanda's exposed flesh as he shakes the can of cream. He breaks off the cap and sprays circles of cream around her nipples and a zigzagging trail from her breasts to her sweet wet spot. Harold slowly starts slurping and kissing off the white sugary goodness from Amanda's soft supple, golden skin. She moans with each soft kiss applied to her freshly bathed skin. The kisses send electric jolts throughout her body. He continues sopping whipped cream from off of his Puerto Rican fantasy as he removes the rest of his attire. Within seconds, he is completely disrobed and ready to give her what she has been anticipating. He finishes with the cream and then submerges his mouth into her wet throbbing love patch. Amanda's moans get louder and she begins to squirm. His tongue motions clear all other thoughts out of her mind. The head is so good that it is all she can focus on. It has completely consumed her mind. She grabs at Harold's hair as he passionately French kisses her throbbing juicy pussy.

"Oh shit baby I'm ready!" She exclaims in a heavy, breathy tone.

"You're not ready till I say you're ready." Harold responds in an authoritative manner. He loves to be in control. He continues as she releases his hair and alternates to gripping the hotel bedding. Amanda is on the verge of an explosion, when Harold stops. Her build up abruptly comes to a halt.

"Fuck!" She exhales as she regains control over herself. Harold brings himself up from Amanda's moist fertile playground. He slips on a condom and penetrates her honey pot. She quivers as he enters. Erotic energy crashes onto Amanda as Harold dives deeper into her love/lust pit. Their movements are slow and synchronized. They move to the rhythm of unadulterated lust. She shakes with every stroke of penetration. Sweat trickles down his forehead and back, as he vigorously moves between her thighs. He dominates her with his technique. Every single movement sends a surge of electricity through her vessel.

After an eternity of passion, she erupts in a fit of orgasmic pleasure. She clings to the sheets for dear life as her body shakes and shutters from the impact of satisfaction. The minutes fly by as he drills between her walls. Tears fall from her face as she takes in short shallow breaths. Then in a climatic instance, he releases his penned up tension.

Harold and Amanda lie in the aftermath of passion. Amanda's head swirls with euphoric emotions. She knows that what she is feeling is real. She does not care about the consequences of her actions. She is ready to leave Carl. She is done with being an unhappily married woman.

"I love you baby!" She blurts out, clearly not thinking about the ramifications of such a statement. Harold, caught off guard by Amanda's confession of love does not know how to respond. Even though he feels something similar, he is not sure if he should say it back. In spite of their troublesome situation, he honestly feels true love for the very first time.

"I love you too Amanda." He utters as he finally acknowledges his feelings. After letting her know they have mutual feelings, he gets up and goes to the shower. She follows him. They spend a loving moment in the shower before preparing themselves both physically and mentally for the return to their less than satisfactory lives.

7:31pm: Harold and Amanda leave the hotel. He walks her to her car and they kiss and embrace before he walks back to his vehicle and leaves.

8:02pm: Harold arrives at Stacy's house. He calls Britney's

cell phone.

"Hey Honey bear, I'm here." He says as she answers.

"Okay Papa bear, I'll be out shortly." His daughter responds. He looks at himself in the mirror. He feels bad but good at the same time. He secretly hopes that neither one of his daughters will end up with a man like himself. He would die if they ever found out about his double life. He loves them too much to hurt them. He tries to rationalize his behavior as he sits alone in his idling BMW. A few minutes later, his daughter Britney comes out. He straightens himself up before she enters the car.

"Hey honey, how was your day?" Harold asks as he studies his daughter. She favors her mother so much. Her bright green eyes and light brown hair, instantly invokes the thought in Harold's mind. He cannot help but to think about Denise. He maintains a smile to hide the guilt that he is feeling.

"My day was pretty awesome; me and Stacy finished the group project. We are going to totally ace it!" Britney responds excitedly. He is so proud of her. She's growing up so fast, he shutters at the thought of her dating. He knows that he only has a couple more years until doomsday, the day Denise and himself agreed to let her begin dating. He pushes those thoughts aside and remembers the gift he purchased for her. He reaches under his seat, and pulls out the "All Boys" combo pack.

"Here you go honey." He says with a smile on his face as he hands her the gift.

"Oh wow you remembered! Thanks Dad!" She exclaims

before giving him a big hug.

"You're welcome honey. You've earned it. I'm proud of you. You're doing so well in school it's the least I could do. It's just my way of saying keep up the good work Honey bear."

"I will dad, I promise!" Britney blurts as she gushes with joy. He put the car in reverse and they start their trip home.

8:20pm: Harold and Britney arrive home. As they enter the house, Harold remembers the letter he received earlier. The thought of it makes him cringe. He knows that he has to get out of the marriage before Denise finds out about everything. As Harold steps into the front room, Janice runs to him and wraps her little arms around his much larger frame. "Daddy," she blurts as she continues to embrace her hero. Harold picks up his precocious little one.

"Hi Honey bunny, Daddy missed you!" He states as he holds her in his arms. "So what did you do today?" He asks as he places her back down and stares into her big gray eyes, her long brown hair, neatly bunched into a ponytail.

"I went to school and I came home, and colored. I made you a picture too Papa Bear!" She says in her cute small voice.

"Oh wow really, I would love to see it." He responds before she runs out of the room. She returns seconds later with a crude homemade picture. The picture is of a stickman with a tie and scribbled black hair. The stickman is sitting in an office with a big window, and a large yellow colored sun with a smiley face drawn on it. "This is a nice picture, do you mind if I take it to work and hang it up in my office?" Harold asks as he stares at the artwork.

"Sure Dad, of course you can. I made it for you!"

"Okay now how about you get ready for bed. And once you're ready, I'll come and read you a bedtime story."

"Alright Papa Bear," she responds before ripping out of the room.

After their children are asleep, Harold and Denise engage in an act of lustful sex. The bustier helps Harold stay focused on his fantasy, Amanda. In the back of her head, Denise knows that she should have insisted that Harold wear a condom. She knows that he has been unfaithful but she just can't will herself to do such a thing. His raw strokes feel so good that part of her deems it a justifiable risk. After a lengthy emotional and mental debate, she gives in and lets lust take control. She gives in to the warmth of his body, the smell of his masculinity, the rhythm of his labor.

In an instant, his raw love makes her succumb to the euphoric ecstasy that only it can induce. Tears fall from her eyes as Harold continues thrusting himself inside of her warm wet walls. Deep down she wants to believe him or rather, she wants to believe in him. She wants to have faith in what he claims, but regardless of how she feels, she knows it is over and the moment that they are sharing, is only a temporary fix. It is merely an illusion of their former relationship, a relationship that has long since died. Her biggest hindrances in breaking away from him are the children, the love she has for him, and his irresistible sexual charm. He has her under control mentally, emotionally, and physically. He has her under his thumb.

DAY 2

8:02am: Harold leaves his house adorned in golfing attire. He leaves his Cranberry BMW, and opts to take his silver S-class Mercedes Benz instead. Malcolm is parked a few houses up the street. He watches as Harold gets in the silver Benz and pulls out of the driveway. Malcolm revs up his car and follows him. He is determined to get enough evidence by week's end.

8:21am: Harold arrives at Grover Lane Apartments. A female comes out of the apartment. Her dark brown skin leggy frame and fashionista flair instantly arouses Malcolm's curiosity. Even in golfer wear, she is still a stunning sight. Her makeup and hair are flawless and her smile looks like it can capture rays of sunlight. Harold always the perfect gentleman gets out and opens the passenger door for her. They share a quick passionate kiss before she gets in his vehicle. As they leave the apartment complex, Malcolm follows not far behind. Harold's female companion is Vicki Phillips. Harold is fifteen years her senior. He knows that their relationship is a temporary fling, so he does not have any feelings invested into it. He only has feelings for one woman, and it's not Denise. He contemplates dropping Vicki back off and contacting Amanda. His heart yearns for her. He finally understands what it means to be in love. The fact that she is still with Carl puts a halt on his plans of being exclusive. He decides to stop thinking about his love and focuses on the day at hand.

8:43am: Harold and Vicki, arrive at "Solon Golf Ways" golf course in Tree Bridge Heights. For the next forty-five minutes or so, the two lust birds kiss, flirt, and half-ass their way through the course. Malcolm captures every single inappropriate kiss, touch, and grope. Harold's prowess to juggle the opposite sex amazes Malcolm.

9:31am: Harold and Vicki leave the golf course. Vicki can barely keep her hands off Harold. She starts by softly massaging his thigh, and ends up giving him a hand job. For the most part, Harold maintains control of the vehicle, only swerving a few times during the trip. Malcolm takes notice of the swerving and can only imagine what is occurring in the car. Vicki continues stoking Harold's stiff hard manhood. Harold enjoys every stroke of her hand.

"If you make it come up, you're going to have to clean it up." He warns as he maintains his composure and keeps the vehicle cruising at a moderately steady speed.

"I always clean up when I'm done playing." She wittily shoots back.

"Touché, that's a good girl." Harold murmurs as he flashes a lustful smile at Vicki. He feels his climax level rising as she increases the passion of her strokes. "Oh yeah baby, I'm about to cum!" He blurts out in a quick breathy tone. Vicki responds by quickly pulling a hanker chief out of her purse and catching Harold's oozing load.

"Aah," Harold moans as the car swerves slightly from his brief loss of control. "Whew fuck!" He exclaims as a big smile forms on his face. Vicki finishes the clean up, and places Harold partially limp penis back into his pants.

9:52am: Harold and Vicki make a stop at a coffee shop on Grand street called "Palace of Beans". Malcolm manages to find a parking spot with a suitable view of the shop. He films as much as possible. Harold is oblivious to Malcolm. He is so engrossed in Vicki, that he barely pays attention to anything else.

"So what do you want to do after we leave from here?" Vicki asks as she drinks her Café Mocha.

"It's up to you baby, it's your special day. We can do whatever; it's all about pleasing you." Harold responds as he carefully sips his French Vanilla

"Well how about we go back to my place and you show me just how much you're willing to please me." Vicki says as she flashes a quick lust infused smile.

"Okay, I'm all for it. It's only fair that you get yours too." Harold murmurs in between sips of his steamy hot beverage.

"That's what I like about baby. You really know how to treat a girl." Vicki responds, totally smitten by his pleasing personality.

10:13am: Harold and Vicki leave the coffee shop. Malcolm gets more footage of the happy lustful couple. Still amazed by the dark brown beauty, Malcolm finds himself entertaining thoughts of sampling her brown sugar. He feels himself starting to dislike Harold even more. He can hardly wait for the prick to get what he deserves. Harold and the luscious Vicki get back in the Silver Benz and head off.

10:41am: They arrive back at the apartment complex. Harold swiftly parks his car. He and Vicki head towards the apartment with a lustful since of urgency. Once inside the apartment, Harold grabs Vicki, and hoists her onto his waist. They kiss and fondle as they make their way up the stairs. Primal instinct has taken control. They are lost in the wiles of lust. The fires of their passion roar as they reach the top of the stairs. Vicki fumbles around in her purse for the keys, while she and Harold continue getting hot and heavy. She finally manages to find them tucked underneath her makeup bag and various scraps of paper. They clumsily make their way to the door of her apartment suite, and after a few distracted attempts, she successfully unlocks it.

Once inside, they rip off each other's clothing in a fit of pure uninhibited lust. Their lust quickly escalates into a burning, all consuming wild fire. Harold carries his chocolate treat into the bedroom. In the bedroom, Vicki gets on her knees and takes Harold's manhood into her warm salivating mouth. She forms a tight smooth grip around his penis with her soft full lips. The moistness of her mouth makes Harold's knees slightly buckle. She bobs her head back and forth on his impressively sized unit. She takes it in deep and feels her involuntary gag reflex kicking in. After a few moments of enjoyment, Harold picks Vicki up and forces her onto the bed.

"I told you that it was about me pleasing you," he utters in a smooth bass tinged voice, before pouncing like a tiger catching its prey. He spreads and lifts her long brown legs apart, and begins his oral assault on her secret garden. His tongue passionately strokes her clitoris, alternating between circular and vertical motions. When her flowers are ready to bloom, he stops and instructs her to bend over the bed. Her top half rests on the bed, while he props her bottom half into the desired position. His forcefulness further stimulates her already engaged sex drive. Harold quickly slides on a condom, and thrusts his hard pulsating cock, balls deep into Vicki's chocolate, juicy snatch.

"Oh fuck!" She yells out in profane approval. Harold thrusts away inside of her tight wet box. She digs her nails into her silk sheets and squirts her love as he continues drilling for pleasure. Her legs shake as her liquid lust runs down them. Harold is satisfying her just right. Vicki moans louder and louder as she sinks deeper and deeper into the pit of pleasure. Harold works her body like a double shift in a steel mill, hard and diligent. He is determined to leave his mark in her memory. He wants to make certain that she will reminisce about him for the rest of her natural life. Suddenly, like an act of a higher power, she dies sexually in an orgasmic fit. Her whole body shakes and tremors as he continues to stroke in her afterlife. He thrusts like a mighty thunder God. Vicki is completely out of it. From this day forward, until another champion lover replaces him, Harold is the best that she has ever had. He finishes and lets out a loud manly grunt. He gets his bearings, and exits her play land.

After taking a shower and getting dressed, Harold kisses Vicki, (who is now fast asleep), and leaves her apartment.

12:05pm: Harold leaves the apartment building. Malcolm being ever so diligent, films every second of every step that Harold makes toward his car. Harold gets in his car and starts it up. Before he leaves the parking lot, his phone begins to ring. He looks at the phone's screen and sees Amanda's number. He quickly answers.

"Hello,"

"Hi sexy, I wanna see you right now." Amanda says in a seductive voice.

"That sounds great baby, but now isn't a good time. I'm in the middle of something. How about I call you back once I get free?" Harold says as a means of stalling. He already knows what she wants, what she longs for. She longs to get fucked, long, and hard.

"Okay well don't keep me waiting too long, I need you Daddy." She states in a brazen sexual manner.

"Alright so what did you have in mind?" He inquires, as he tries to block out thoughts of Vicki's moans, sex faces, and irresistible frame. It is at this moment, that he comes to the realization that he can't do it anymore. He can't continue juggling multiple women. It has to end. Time is no longer on his side. The grays of wisdom are starting to creep in, and Karma is not far behind.

"A little of this and a little of that, I'm going to be at the Super Eight on Aurora Boulevard, room six. Don't keep me waiting too long." Amanda says with eagerness present in her voice.

"I won't, I promise." Harold responds as he turns the corner and hits a main intersection. "Give me like forty minutes, I'll be there."

12:35pm: Harold pulls into the parking lot of the Super 8 motel, with his tail not far behind. Malcolm is astonished by the fact that Harold just left Vicki's apartment and is now about to meet someone else at a motel.

"Talk about sexual addiction!" Malcolm mumbles as he gets his camera ready. "He's definitely here to see another chick. This guy is fucking disgrace!" He says aloud as he watches the latest part of Harold's extramarital saga. Harold parks his car and calls Amanda.

"I'm here." Harold utters into the phone as he heads to room six. Amanda opens the door just as Harold reaches it. Malcolm zooms in on them before Harold enters the room. He gets an excellent shot of them kissing before Harold goes in.

"It's about time you got here Papi I was starting to get lonely." Amanda says as she rubs Harold's chest.

"Why so impatient senorita, good things come to those who wait." Harold responds as he lustfully scopes Amanda's lovely physique, in her tight revealing dark red mini dress.

"Well I've been waiting, so now I want that good thing!" Amanda says before planting her lips on Harold's lips and forcing her tongue inside of his mouth. Harold responds with mutual vigor. He forces Amanda up against the wall closest to the door. His hands fondle her luscious frame. They glide from her shapely legs, to underneath her dress. His fingers make contact with her bare, uncovered moist snatch.

"Surprise no panties." She says in an ultra seductive voice. He smiles in response and quickly undoes his pants. He throws caution to the wind, spreads her legs, and shoves his erect cock into her moist chocha.

"I Papi," Amanda exclaims as the hard warm penis thrusts into her sugar walls. Harold grabs both of her legs, hoists her up on his waist, and commences to fuck her roughly against the drab wallpaper covered wall. Lacking a condom, her wetness is much more intense than before. He feels her bare insides; every stroke draws him deeper into the act of copulation. He tries his best to convey his deep longing affection for her. In one swift motion, he lifts her from off of the wall and walks her over to the bed; all the while, still pumping away. His sexual prowess is indeed above average. He rests her on the edge of the bed and props her legs on his shoulders. He continues hammering away in passionate rhythmic motions. She moans louder and louder, as her champion lover controls the situation.

"Oh fuck! I-I love you!" Amanda shouts as Harold fucks her sweet tight twat like a wild man.

"Yeah baby cum for Daddy!" He commands as he has his way with her.

"Oh Papi, I'm almost there, Aah!" Amanda yells as her legs twitch against Harold. His now sweat soaked shirt sticks to his defined chest as he wails away at his object of desire. "Here it comes! Oh!" Amanda moans before her volcano erupts. Her body vibrates as an instant effect of climatic pleasure. Harold feels himself nearing completion, and quickly slips out. He explodes over the outside of her fun zone.

"Better out than in… fuck!" He mumbles as he continues his release. He looks down at Amanda and sees Vicki! He shakes his head in disbelief. He looks back again, and sees Denise! He quickly closes his eyes. Amanda notices his weird behavior and addresses it.

"Are you okay?" She inquires as she reaches for something to catch Harold's now dripping load. Harold looks back at her and sees, just Amanda.

"Yeah… I'm okay. I just got little dizzy." He utters as he

realizes the effect that his behavior is having on his psyche. He is lost in the sinful debacle that has become his life. His haphazard lifestyle has become an all-consuming addiction. He is blatantly in denial. He still thinks that he is in control but in reality, he is completely lost. His lack of self-control is now comparable to that of a person addicted heavily to a vice. The kind that believes that they can quit anytime they desire to do so. His nose is wide open. He is desperately in need of an intervention. Amanda takes a moment for herself, while Harold rushes into the shower. She thinks about what has just occurred. She knows what she has to do. She has to end it today. She has to leave Carl! Amanda hears the water from the shower start up as she lies across the bed. She contemplates staying for the night and dealing with Carl tomorrow. She can no longer deal with the arguing and fighting. She is tired of using lies and excuses to hold on to an already failed marriage. She no longer wants to be the villainess. Carl has every right to act the way he acts. He is the victim. He is the one left with the trick, while she gets the treat. Amanda builds up her courage, and grabs her phone from off of the nightstand. Her anxiety level rises with each digit dialed. She feels a knot form in her stomach as she waits for Carl to answer.

"Amanda?" Carl says as he answers the phone. His mind is hazy, courtesy of marijuana.

"Yeah, it's me… um… I have to tell you something." She has been planning this day for weeks. She even made sure to take a week's worth of clothing and personal items. She waited until Carl fell asleep before hastily gathering her things and slipping out. Carl waits in silence on the other end of the line while Amanda struggles to finish her statement. His mind is already thinking the worst and the paranoia induced by the weed, only amplifies his already dreadful thoughts.

"What, are we done?" He inquires, breaking the silence and helping the process along.

"Yeah, well…I…I can't do this anymore. I'm sick of arguing, I'm sick of the weed, the cigarettes, and your lack of motivation. You say you want to make things better, but your lack of action tells me something different. I'm not coming home tonight. We're through…" Amanda's words trail off and the silence sets back in. Carl, still in a catatonic stupor is slow to react. He was already somewhat expecting to hear it. It's been a long time coming.

"What…why? I mean…why can't we work it out? I love you," Is all that he can force himself to say. He wonders if that is in fact her true reason or if she is being unfaithful.

"Look, it's done. I'm done! You're hindering me, bringing me down—"

"Who is he?" Carl blurts out, cutting Amanda off like a car in traffic.

"What are you talking about? Didn't you hear everything I just said?" She questions as she contemplates revealing the truth.

"I heard what you just said, but did you hear what I just asked you? WHO IS HE?" His voice elevates with a harsh undertone.

"It doesn't matter, what matters is the fact that I'm done!"

Amanda hears Harold shutting off the water. "I gotta go, don't try to find me…I'll be back for my things by the end of the week." She says before abruptly ending the conversation. At that moment, Harold emerges from the bathroom with nothing but a towel on. His glistening ripped body excites Amanda. She pictures herself waking up to him morning after morning for the rest of her natural life. She is in love and is ready to take their relationship to the next level. "I broke it off with Carl." She blurts out as she continues to stare at her champion stallion.

"You did what?" Harold responds, completely thrown off by the revelation.

"I…I ended it. I'm done. I only want to be with you. I really want to give us a chance." She confesses, putting it all on the line, placing all or nothing on her sure fire bet.

"Whoa you did what? I…" He pauses as he searches for the right way to convey his thoughts. Unlike Amanda, He knows that his breaks will not be as clean, especially with Denise and his children. Vicki is just a fling of the moment, so he is not too concerned with her; his only concern is his family and wealth. "Baby slow down, I feel the same as you and I'm ready to have a fresh start too but if I leave my wife, I stand to lose at least half of everything I've worked for. That's half of the fruits of my labor, half of my blood, sweat, and tears. Now is not the time—" Amanda feels anger starting to rise.

"So what are you saying? Are you trying to say that you're not willing to walk away and have a clean slate because money is involved? I don't know about you, but I'm tired of sneaking around and keeping secrets. I'm ready to commit to you and only you! Harold...I...I love you." Amanda says as she feels her eyes get warm with emotion. She doesn't want Harold to see her cry, but she can't help it. She's in love and ready to devote her all to him.

"Hold on honey, I didn't mean it like that...I love you too, it's just that...well the money doesn't mean as much as the impression that it will leave on my daughters. I want to have a fresh start...I want to be able to just run off with you and start anew. I really do but in all honesty...I need a little bit of time." Harold says as he watches the first few tears run down Amanda's rosy red cheeks. He rushes over to comfort her and they spend a few moments in silence. Harold holds her tight as he starts to feel tears forming in his own eyes. Time stops as they sit alone in room six of the budget motel, crying, comforting one another, and both wishing that things were not so complicated. After some time has lapsed, Harold breaks the silence. "Just give me a week." He murmurs, not particularly sure of what he's committing to. He is formulating off the cuff. "I'm leaving Denise in a week." He states flatly, devoid of any emotion. He knows what he has to do. The gears are in motion. There is no turning back. He does not want to lose the best thing that has ever happened to him. He does not want to lose Amanda.

"Are you sure about that?" Amanda questions, as she looks into Harold's eyes.

"Yes, I'm positive. I'm ready to be happy." He says with a smile. Amanda and Harold share one last passionate kiss before he gets dressed.

1:45pm: Harold leaves room six. Malcolm, on the verge of falling asleep barely notices him. He only manages to get a couple of shots of Harold walking back to his car. Thoughts cloud Harold's mind as he gets into his vehicle. He is a troubled man. His heart is heavy and his conscience is eating him alive. He contemplates if true love is worth losing millions. Even if the courts did award Denise with half of his wealth, he would still have enough to maintain a comfortable lifestyle and his business would supply him with a nice stream of future earnings. He is so absorbed in his thoughts that he again fails to notice Malcolm. He starts up his luxury car and heads home.

2:31pm: Harold arrives back home. He tries his best to block out everything. He goes in the house and puts on the facade of a happy loving husband. He sees Denise in the kitchen and heads straight towards her. She is in the middle of juicing some new concoction that she more than likely got off some daytime talk show or weblog. She was once a shopaholic, but that got old after a couple of years. So now, she is more of a homebody. TV and the internet has become her life. She has so many shows recorded on her DVR; it is a wonder that she finds time to watch them all. "Judge Judy", "America's Next Top Model", and "The Wendy Williams Show", are just some of the shows frequently captured on it. Harold slowly creeps up behind her and grabs her around the waist. She involuntarily jumps and lets out a short shriek.

"Harold!" She snaps as she turns around to see the man that was once the love of her life but is now the cause of her heartache.

"Hey baby, I missed you," he responds before kissing her.

"You missed me? I'm surprised considering how busy you've been lately." She retorts, clearly expressing her disdain for his frequent absence and negligence.

"Yes, I missed you silly! I've been thinking…how about we have a nice family night out, just you, the girls, and me. We could go catch a movie and maybe have a bite to eat afterwards." His family night request really throws her for a loop. She wonders if maybe he's feeling guilty or if he genuinely wants to make up for lost time. It's hard to tell with a man like Harold. Denise has never found any telltale marks or evidence to substantiate her suspicions of infidelity; no scratches, hickies, or unaccounted for periods of time, no clothing, makeup, or other personal items from other females, left in any of his cars. She has even gone as far as checking his phone every night for an entire month! Unbeknownst to Denise, Harold keeps a second prepaid phone stashed away and goes to great lengths to keep his vehicles and body evidence free. Harold has been unfaithful almost as long as they have been married! He knows all of the ins and outs. He has mastered the art of deception. Hiding his sexual dalliances from Denise has become second nature. Most of them have never lasted longer than three months. Harold gets bored easily with the majority of the ones he attracts. Quite a few of them were like Vicki, young, naïve, and easily blinded by money. Amanda is something different; she has something that captures his full attention. There is a factor she possesses, which makes it close to impossible for him to let her go. Even when Carl found out about their affair the first time around, they still managed to keep a slight connection. It took a lot of money and a fall guy to keep Denise from getting wind of it. Even after all of that, he still chooses to carry on with it. Their relationship breaks almost every rule in his book and goes drastically against his better judgment. "So what do you say? Are you up for it?" He questions while forcing a slightly exaggerated smile.

"Well, I guess. I mean it's not like we get a chance to do things together often." Denise agrees. She figures that it will be good for the kids to see them together and for them all to have a good time. It has been ages since they have had a family outing.

3:32pm: Harold and his family leave the house. They hop into a black Cadillac Escalade and pull out of the driveway. Malcolm figures that it would be a good time to catch a break. He starts up his car and heads out to get a bite to eat.

DAY 3

"Hi honey, I'll be home in a bit. I'm just going out with the guys to a have a couple of beers okay?" Harold says on the phone to his wife as he pulls up to Grover Lane apartments. He has done this type of thing so many times that it has become second nature. Part of him somewhere deep down knows it's wrong, but his very essence yearns for the thrill of being unfaithful and getting away with it. He steps out of his cranberry red BMW and walks up to the apartment building. He has the confidence and prowess of a seasoned veteran. He is like an MVP athlete; he knows how to play the field like the back of his hand. He knows every lie, every alibi, what gifts will smooth things over when situations get hairy, and most importantly, he knows how to pull out and not get too involved. He thinks that he knows it all, but he is still unaware of Malcolm. He watches as Harold's fingers gracefully glide over the security system's keypad. Malcolm records him effortlessly pick the four numbers to gain access to his jackpot. Within seconds,

Vicki answers.

"Hello," she says in a sweet sensuous manner.

"Hey baby, it's me," Harold responds in a smooth cocky tone.

"Okay sexy I'm buzzing you in right now. I'll be on my way down in a minute." Vicki responds before a loud buzzer begins screaming. Harold pulls the door open and casually strolls inside of the lobby area. Within a matter of minutes, he can see a pair of long luscious legs gracefully make their way down towards him. The rest of the package is equally as stunning. She is a sweet temptation that Harold is ready to indulge. *"I'm really going to miss having fun with her."* He thinks as he continues to stare at the gorgeous dark beauty. She greets him with a warm smile and an even warmer hug. He feels his manly senses awaken as he embraces her flawless frame.

"So you couldn't wait till seven huh?" She asks as she continues to smile at the handsomely devilish Harold.

"Well when you have gifts under the tree, you always want to wake up early to open them right?" He responds with flirtatious charm.

"Whoa tiger, save that for later," she responds while grabbing his hand. Malcolm bears witness yet again to Harold exiting the building in the company of Vicki. He escorts her to his car and opens the passenger door for her like a perfect gentleman.

6:54pm: The handsome couple arrives at "Toni's". He lets Vicki out of the car and hands off the keys to the valet. After passing off the keys, he opens the restaurant door and escorts her inside. Once inside, he makes eye contact with James. James already knows the routine.

"Hello and welcome to Toni's. How may I help you?" He says as he puts on the whole routine all the while laughing in his head. He has done it so many times that he is amazed that Harold still manages to find new women. *"This guy has probably banged half of the city!"* He thinks as he waits for Harold's routine response.

"Hello James my name is Harold and I have a reservation for two." He says while flashing the same fake plastered on smile like many times before. James shows them to Harold's "special" booth and returns back to the greeter podium. Harold contemplates whether he should break it off over diner or keep it going and have one last moment of intimacy later at her apartment. Thoughts of Amanda's decision replay in his head. The memory of them crying together in the motel room haunts him. Her leaving Carl has really complicated things. He feels guilty as he stares across the table at Vicki. Wanting to appease both his physical and emotional needs, he decides to end things with Vicki after one last roll in the hay.

"I had a great time yesterday. You're starting to be like a drug, I'm getting addicted to you." Vicki says as she stares into Harold's grayish blue eyes. Harold is lost in deep thought. Things are definitely starting to bother him. For the first time in years, his conscience is really getting the best of him. "Hello? Are you alright?" Vicki asks, snapping Harold out of his trance-like state.

"Yeah I'm good. I'm just a little tired from work." He responds as a waitress arrives to take their order.

"Hello welcome to Toni's. My name is Jennifer and I will be your waitress for this evening. What would you like to drink?" She asks as she hands them both menus. Jennifer tries to keep her focus on the both of them and not just Harold but his strikingly handsome looks make it a challenge to say the least. She manages to break his intoxicating spell and shifts her focus to his flawless date. The dark dazzling beauty with flawless black short cut hair is a sharp contrast to her pale dull skin, bleached split ends, and chipped nail polish. She knows that the chances of a man like Harold noticing a girl like her are slimmer than an anorexic supermodel.

"Hello Jennifer. Well for starters, we would like a bottle of 1998 Veuve Clicquot La Grande Dame. We would also like an order of Shrimp Rillettes."

"Okay sir I will be right back with your bottle and appetizers." Jennifer says before walking away. Vicki is impressed with his choices. She loves the way he takes control and handles things.

"So where do you see this going?" Vicki asks as she looks intensely at Harold. He hates when a woman asks that question. It usually means that she wants to be a bigger part of his life. It also means that she has some doubts about what he wants. Harold hates this part and always tries to avoid it because once they reach this point, they begin to attach and invest themselves emotionally. He seriously has second thoughts about one last sexual encounter.

"Well it's still fairly early in our situation and at the moment, I can't really say. I don't want to say something misleading or make a commitment. I mean, we're still getting to know one another. I have a three month rule and the rule is to wait until the end of the third month to decide whether to take it to the next level or call it quits." Vicki is a little disappointed in his response, but she respects his honesty.

"Okay I respect your honesty. I really do but that's not what I wanted to hear. I mean, it's been magical between us and I'm really feeling what we have. The spontaneity, the excitement, and you have a sense of class about you that many of the men I've dealt with don't." Vicki places her hand on Harold's hand. "Look baby, all I'm saying is that…I don't want to let go of something so good. I don't want to let go of you." Vicki's words hit Harold like a freight train.

"Damn it's too late! She's in too deep!" Harold thinks as he feels the warmth of Vicki's hand resting on top of his. He wants to pull out and cut the date short. He wants to call Amanda. He is ready to quit his games and come clean. Jennifer comes back with their bottle of wine and appetizers. She notices the mood at the table has changed.

"Are you ready to order?" She inquires as she shifts her attention back to doing her job.

"Uh yes, give me the Steak and Shrimp Scampi Medley with steamed broccoli and white rice. Also, I want the steak medium rare and my lovely lady will have—"

"I will have a sautéed chicken breast and a side of shrimp

49

Scampi with rice pilaf." Vicki interjects.

"Okay. I will be right back with your meals." Jennifer says before grabbing their menus and leaving.

"So are we cool?" Harold asks, sensing dissention between them. He opens up the bottle of wine, and fills both of their glasses.

"Yeah we're fine, just fine." Vicki says before gulping down a considerable portion of her wine. The tone of her voice has changed significantly. Harold understands that his response to her inquiry, has rubbed her the wrong way. He sips some of his wine as he thinks of what he really wants to do with her. He wants to have a little more fun before he relinquishes his access to her. The rest of the dinner goes off without a hitch. They enjoy their food, and keep the conversation to a minimum. The more Vicki drinks, the less upset she becomes.

"So are you ready for dessert?" Harold asks as he finishes his meal.

"No not really. I just want to go back to my place and get fucked." Vicki says bluntly. "So are we gonna fuck or what?" She questions. Her straight forwardness catches Harold completely off guard. It is exactly what he wants, sex and no feelings.

"Okay, as soon as I get the check we're out." He responds, blocking out thoughts of Amanda and replacing them with thoughts of fucking Vicki. He fantasizes about having Vicki's long legs wrapped around him as he pounds her sweet in between. Jennifer returns to the table.

"So would you care for any dessert?" She asks as she clears off the table.

"No, we're done. Can you bring us the check?" Harold responds as he anticipates getting in Vicki's panties for one last hurrah.

"Okay sir, I will be right back with it." Jennifer says before hurrying off.

After paying for the meals and leaving Jennifer and James significant tips, Harold and Vicki leave "Toni's". They are both feeling the effects of being slightly inebriated, Vicki more so.

7:47pm Harold and Vicki are seen exiting the restaurant and waiting for the valet. Malcolm starts up his car and continues recording. The valet attendant returns a few moments later with Harold's car. As usual, he lets Vicki in before himself. Once he is in, they speed off into the night with Malcolm following behind like a shadow.

Inside the cranberry colored BMW, erotic music plays through the customized BOSE sound system. Vicki gets hornier by minute. She is hurt. The only thing she wants is a good fuck and some much needed rest. She wishes that she had her very own special someone to ease her lonely nights but is willing to make due with a few moments of pleasure instead.

"Now when we get in, I want straight fucking. I don't want any kissing, soft touching, or cuddling. I just want you to fuck the shit outta me and then be on your way." Vicki says in a slightly slurred manner. She feels no love. The hurt has brought on the lust bug big time. Harold does not respond. He just keeps his eyes focused on the road and wonders if he heard her correctly. "Did you hear me? I want you to fuck the shit out of this black wet pussy! I want you to make me cum all over your hard white dick!" Vicki's aggressiveness is really starting to turn him on. He can hardly wait to oblige her demands.

"I heard you loud and clear. I'm going to fuck the shit out of that black pussy!" Harold proclaims with absolute confidence.

8:22pm: Harold's car pulls into Vicki's apartment complex. He parks and wastes no time getting Vicki out. Once inside her apartment, they get right down to business. Harold lifts Vicki and carries her into the bedroom. He does not even waste time removing her panties. He moves them to the side and lets his fingers warm her up. He fingers her aggressively. He rubs his thumb back and forth over Vicki's clitoris, while plunging his middle finger in and out of her sweet nectar pit. Vicki moans loudly in approval as he continues to warm her up. Vicki writhes and shakes as Harold titillates her sweet spot. His efforts are fruitful; she pops into a climatic seizure and squirts all over the sheets.

"Oh fuck!" She exhales as she catches her breath. Her legs shake uncontrollably as Harold gets his now hard dick ready for penetration. He effortlessly slides on a condom and dives into her wet, throbbing treasure-trove. She continues to moan and shake as Harold fucks her hard and steady. She screams as he rails her. She loves every rough intense moment of it.

"Do you like the way I'm fucking your sweet pussy?" He questions in an overtly dominating tone.

"Hell yeah, Fuck this pussy Daddy!" She responds, completely enjoying the moment. He continues banging her walls with reckless abandonment. She groans, howls, and grips the sheets as if possessed by a legion of demons. He gives her a few more heavy concentrated thrusts and they both reach the top of the mountain.

"Oh fuck Daddy, thank you!" She releases in a breathy, shaky voice.

"No thank you." Harold responds as he slides out of her. They are both satisfied with having their physical needs met. Harold wipes the sweat from off of his forehead and goes into the bathroom for a quick clean up before heading home.

9:12pm: Harold walks out of the apartment building. Malcolm on the verge of dosing off quickly shakes off the drowsiness and fumbles to get his recording device running. He successfully gets most of Harold's journey from the apartment to his car. Considering the quietness of the parking lot, he waits until Harold begins driving before starting up his car.

9:49pm: Harold pulls into his driveway, powers off his second cell phone, and stashes it before going into the house. He is happy and relaxed. Vicki was exactly what he needed to clear the space in his complicated mess of a mind. He contemplates calling Amanda before stepping inside but decides that it would better if he waited until tomorrow.

DAY 4

9:05am: After settling in for another day at the office, Harold receives a call on his second cell phone.

"Hey baby. I can't wait to see you today." Amanda says in a happy upbeat tone.

"I was just about to call you. Are you still at the motel?" He asks as he checks through a series of urgent emails.

"Well right now I'm at work but I'll be staying at Alicia's house until next week. I'm going to pick up all of my stuff from the house tomorrow."

"So how did Carl take it?"

"I'm not really sure but I'm guessing not too well. I haven't talked to him since I broke it off. I called him this morning but he didn't answer."

"Okay…so what do you think is going on with him, you don't think he tried to kill himself do you?" Even though he has taken Carl's wife, Harold still has no ill will towards him, especially considering the complexity of their situation.

"I doubt it. I've never known him to be the suicidal type, even when things weren't going right. You've known him longer than me, so I should be asking you that question instead."

"Well, I mean...yeah you do have a point." Harold's conscience really starts to fuck with him as he thinks about his broken relationship with Carl. A spike of remorse resounds deep inside of him. He knows that his status and financial stability have contributed greatly to his lack of consideration for others. He has second thoughts in regards to what he is about to tell Amanda. He is about to make major choices that will greatly affect her life as well as his own. "Okay let's not think about that anymore. All it's going to do is cloud our judgment and hinder us from finding true happiness. I have quite a few things that I need to discuss and come clean to you about. What time do you go to lunch today?" Harold is ready to disclose his fling with Vicki and announce his plans of Amanda and himself getting their own place together.

"I go to lunch at twelve but I can probably sneak out ten minutes earlier. Did you want to meet up?"

"Yes, I really need to tell you what's on my mind." Harold says as he feels a huge weight starting to lift from off of his shoulders.

"Okay baby. I'll be there at twelve on the dot." Amanda responds before the call ends. The wheels are in motion. The next thing on Harold's agenda is to break it off with Vicki.

11:59am: Amanda pulls up in front of Harold office. Like clockwork, Harold emerges from the building. He quickly hops in her car and they head off. Malcolm has decided that after today, he should have enough evidence for Spellman to present to Denise. Even though he does not have actual footage of Harold engaging in sexual acts, he still has enough to make a flawless argument in a divorce proceeding. As usual, he follows the sorry excuse for a man.

12:11pm: Amanda and Harold arrive at a different destination than their previous outings. They arrive at a sandwich-based bar and grill called "Pappy's Bread". Once inside, they take a small table close to a series of large windows. They are in perfect view for filming. Malcolm seizes the opportunity and immediately begins recording.

"So what did you want to tell me?" Amanda inquires as she glosses over the lunch menu. Harold pauses and thinks before speaking. He has a lot to say and does not want any part of it to be misconstrued.

"Well…I thought about our situation…and…I've decided to break the news to my wife tonight. In addition to breaking the news to Denise, I also have to break it off with a fling I was seeing while you were still with Carl. I don't have anything serious with the person but if we're going to start our situation off right, I have to tell you everything. I want us to start with a clean slate. Amanda baby, what I feel with you is something that I've never felt before. The feeling that I have in my heart is something that I need to keep feeling. I don't want it to go away and I don't want you to go away. What I'm saying is that, I want to get serious with you. So much so, that I want us to have our own place together." Harold's announcements, have Amanda completely floored. She doesn't know how to respond. The news is bittersweet. She is ecstatic about Harold being ready to have an official relationship but at the same, she is upset with the fact that he has been having a fling in addition to their adulterous affair. A small inkling of doubt starts to form in her rational mind.

"Wait, so you mean to tell me that you have someone else besides Denise and me?"

"Well yes but it's not what you think. As of today, I'm through with her and every other woman but you."

"Okay that sounds good and all but how can I trust what you're saying? I mean I know that I should be the last person to have doubts considering my own situation but how do I know that you won't do the same thing to me somewhere down the line?" Amanda questions as she continues looking over the menu. Harold understands her reservations and thinks of a way to put her mind at ease.

As Harold is thinking of the perfect choice of words, a waitress approaches their table. She is a petite light skinned female with sandy brown hair. Her bubbly demeanor instantly catches their attention.

"Hello folks. How are ya'll doing? My name is Cassie and I'll be your server for today. What can I start you guys off with, any drinks or appetizers?" Cassie asks in a warm perky manner.

"Hi Cassie I would like the soup and bread lunch special with a small Pepsi." Amanda says while scanning over the young vibrant girl.

"Okay and what type of soup and side salad would you like?"

"Give me the Chicken Soup Surprise and a Caesar salad."

"Alright and what would you like sir," Harold quickly scans the menu and picks the first thing that catches his eye.

"I'll have the Roast Beef French Dip, with a small Greek salad." He murmurs as he second-guesses his decision of divulging his fling.

"Alright let me take these menus and I'll be back in a few with your lunch choices." Cassie says before heading off towards the kitchen.

"Okay so let me get this straight, I give you what you want, and now you're having reservations about us? Are you serious?" Harold inquires while trying to keep his voice from elevating.

"Harold, I just need to know that we're going to have something different from what we're both walking away from. I want to be the only one that gets your heart and great sex from here on out. I'm not sharing you and once we take this step, there is no turning back." Amanda's words are stern and have a deathly seriousness to them. Harold now realizes just how invested she is to the notion of them being a couple.

"Babes, you have my absolute word that from this day forward, it's just you and I. No one else will ever come between us. I'm done with cheating. The way that you make me feel is different from anything I've ever known. Even Denise has never made me feel like this. I don't care if our families have objections about us being together. I don't care if I lose friends because of it. Amanda honey, all I care about is you and your happiness." Harold lets his emotions pour out of his mouth like water breaking free from a dam. He means every word, every syllable. He has truly found love. Harold's declaration has erased all doubt from Amanda's consciousness. She feels the sincerity in each word. She is ready to be happy and run off with her true love. She is ready to have an ending like the fairytales she obsessed over as a child. Her knight in flawed armor has slain the dragon and rescued her heart. Amanda, energized by the love, reaches over and steals a quick kiss from Harold. Malcolm, who is still recording captures it perfectly through the huge front window.

12:47pm: Amanda and Harold arrive back at Harold's office. They kiss and say their goodbyes, before Harold exits the vehicle. Once out of the car, he watches as Amanda heads off. He then takes a quick glance at his surroundings and notices a man that appears to be filming him! Malcolm, realizing that Harold is aware of his presence, gets out of his car and acts as if he's capturing images of the entire street. Harold stares intensely at Malcolm as the gears in his head start working. He knows that he's seen the man before but he can't quite put his finger on where. He contemplates confronting him but doesn't want to seem like some sort of paranoid wacko. Malcolm continues his impromptu performance. He stays calm and avoids eye contact with Harold. After a few moments of indecisiveness, Harold chooses to confront him. Malcolm takes notice of Harold walking towards him and a similar incident comes to mind. He stays calm and prepares for the confrontation.

"Excuse me what are you doing?" Harold inquires in an interrogative manner as he gives Malcolm a stone hard look.

"What are you talking about?" Malcolm plays dumb and gives Harold a blank stare.

"Dude, why are you following me?" Harold's inquiry puts Malcolm on the defense.

"Following you? Why would I be following you? I don't even know who you are!" Malcolm says with a defensive tone in his voice.

"You were following and filming me!" Harold exclaims as his anger starts to build.

"Look fella, I don't know what you're talking about. I'm an artist. I capture real images and turn them into unique pieces of art using a combination of various software programs and real time texture paints." Malcolm has used this cover so many times that he has mastered it from every single angle.

"Okay so if you're an artist you should have samples of your work available for the public to view, am I right?"

"Oh I do," Malcolm responds as he reaches into his pocket and pulls out a mock business card. "Here's my website." He says as he hands Harold the card. "Go on there and check out my stuff." Harold reads the card and is at a loss for words. He is so embarrassed. Images from his childhood come to mind, images of Bugs Bunny morphing into a Jackass during a moment of stupidity. Harold feels the blood rush to his cheeks. He feels like a Jackass indeed.

"Um, okay. I'll check em' out. Sorry about that…" He utters before making a hasty retreat. Malcolm has had enough narrow escapes in his time of being a Private Investigator to know when to wrap it up. He quickly returns to his vehicle and calls up Attorney Spellman. Spellman's secretary answers.

"Spellman and associates Linda speaking, how may I help you?"

"Hey Linda, it's Malcolm Scott, I need to speak with Spellman. Tell him it's urgent."

"Okay, I'm transferring you right now." Linda says before transferring the call.

"Attorney Spellman speaking,"

"Hey Spellman, it's Malcolm, I'm done."

"Are you sure that you have enough on the guy?"

"Yeah, I'm positive. With the footage and pictures that I have, your case against that creep will be foolproof."

"Sounds great, how about you swing by my office in like the next forty minutes, I'll be ready for you by then."

"Alright I gotcha,"

Malcolm arrives at Spellman's office. He is both excited and relieved to be finished with the mess of Harold. The past few days have taken a toll on him. He is both repulsed and in awe of Harold's activeness. He ponders how such a person could be so active and manage not to crash and burn. He has not dealt with something as intense and all consuming in years. He is drained both mentally and physically. The slight red tint of his eyes and the bags under them are telltale signs of sleep deprivation. Now that his task is completed, a long week of rest awaits him. Thanks to the considerable amount of money Spellman paid to retain his services, it is now feasible.

Spellman sits in his office awaiting the meeting with Malcolm. He is anxious to see the evidence that Malcolm has compiled. He loves righting wrongs and adding more money to his already abundant bank account. He has certainly carved out a niche by effectively providing legal representation to high society's unhappily married. His last case alone netted him twenty-five percent of a multimillion-dollar divorce settlement. Thanks to lack of self-control on the part of the wealthy, his years of law school have paid off quite handsomely. Spellman takes notice of his office line flashing and picks up. *"Mr. Spellman, Malcolm is here to see you."*

"Okay thank you send him back." Spellman is giddy with anticipation. His anticipation is comparable to that of a child waiting to open a birthday gift. A knock on the door lets him know that Malcolm has arrived. "Come in," Malcolm enters the room with evidence in hand. "Hello Malcolm, have a seat." Spellman greets his weary guest and they get right down to business.

"Okay here it goes," Malcolm says as he starts up one of the video files. Spellman's eyes light up as he watches the undisputable footage. Thoughts of another victory flash in his head.

"Wow this guy really has quite the sexual appetite." Spellman murmurs as he continues to watch the videos

"Yeah I got exhausted just filming it." Malcolm retorts.
"I don't know how he's managed not to get caught."

"He's probably been doing it so long that he knows exactly what not to do." Harold's abundance in extramarital activity, will make for one of the most exciting cases that Spellman has had privy to in years "This is good stuff what about the photos?" Spellman asks, evidently pleased with the videos.

"Oh yeah those are pretty good too," Malcolm utters before setting up his photo gallery. "Check em' out." The photo gallery shows Harold in various compromising situations, from kissing in Amanda's car, to going in and out of Vicki's apartment.

"Okay well I think we definitely have enough to win the case and get a sizeable settlement. Thank you for your remarkable service. I will definitely do business with you in the future." Spellman shakes Malcolm's hand and shows him out. Once Malcolm has left, Spellman places a call to Denise Atkins. Denise, in the middle of watching an episode of Judge Judy, answers the call.

"Hello?"

"Hello Mrs. Atkins this is Attorney Spellman. I have something that you definitely need to see. How soon can you make it down to my office?"

"Um...well I can make it down after my girls get home from school. How's four sound?" Denise feels a sense of dread creeping over her. She knows that the lawyer has something that will give truth to her intuition.

"Four sounds good. I'll see then."

"Okay," she murmurs as a terrible, sinking feeling begins to form in the pit of her gut. The phrase "Be careful what you wish for because you just might get it," echoes in her head.

Denise parks outside of the office of Spellman and associates. She has second thoughts about going through with it. She doesn't want to know but she needs to know. She needs to know the truth about Harold. She forces herself out of the car. Her legs feel as heavy as lead and her heartbeat is as fast as the fluttering wings of a hummingbird. The closer she gets, the more intense her panic sensations become. She pushes on and manages to make it inside, once inside the drab typical looking attorney's office, her panic symptoms peak. She can barely get out her words as she reaches the receptionist desk. "Uh...hi...I-I'm here to see attorney

Spellman."

"Okay and you are?"

"Denise, Denise Atkins,"

"Alright Denise have a seat. I'll let attorney Spellman know that you're here to see him." Linda pages Spellman. "Hello Mr. Spellman, Denise Atkins is here to see you,"

"Okay Linda, send her back." He responds.

"Mr. Spellman is ready to see you Mrs. Atkins."

"Thank you." Denise responds before making her way to Spellman's office. She reaches Spellman's office and softly knocks on the door.

"Come in," Spellman says in a slightly elevated tone. Denise enters the office and takes a seat. Attorney Spellman greets her and immediately shows her the evidence. Denise's heart breaks as she views the incriminating evidence. She feels sick to her stomach as she watches her husband kiss and grope other women. She almost loses it completely when he walks into Vicki's apartment building.

"That's enough. I don't want to see anymore." She utters as she holds her mouth and she turns away. She fights back her tears and struggles to keep her composure. She feels numb. It feels like someone has just died. Her hands start to shake uncontrollably as she rises from her seat.

"Are you okay?" Spellman asks in a concerned tone.

"Yes, now can you please shut it off?" Spellman closes the programs. "I will let you know when I'm ready to move forward." She says before abruptly rushing out of his office. Denise power walks out of his office. She continues the hurried pace until she reaches her car. Tears run down her face as she starts up the engine. Her world is crashing down around her. She realizes that she has wasted precious amounts of love and devotion on a doomed marriage. Never in a million years would she have thought that the man, in whom she gave her best years to, would end up being the cause of so much heartache. She completely falls to pieces as her car sits with its engine idling. She shuts out the world around her as she releases all of the dark feelings of misery and despair. She finishes her moment of release and realizes what she must now do. Harold has to go. She does not want that type of man setting a horrible example for her precious girls.

Harold is in the middle of a conference call when he receives a text message from Vicki *"Still thinking about last night… ☺ Call me when you get a chance sexy xoxo."* He contemplates texting her back and breaking the news. He finishes handling business and opts to call her instead.

"Hello sexy." Vicki answers in her sweetest, most seductive voice.

"Hey Vicki…uh listen… about last night…"

"Yeah it was great! I need you to give it to me like that more often."

"Well, what I've called to tell you is that there isn't going to be anymore nights like last night. Vicki we're done." Harold murmurs with sincerity.

"What? We're done, what do you mean we're done?" The tone in Vicki's voice changes drastically.

"I mean that I can't do this anymore. The way things went at dinner last night really made me realize that we're not meant for each other. Believe me it's not you it's completely me, I'm set in my ways and—"

"Oh so instead of telling me yesterday during diner, you decide to get one last fuck and then dump me? You're a piece of shit! My sister told me not fuck with your white ass! She told me you wasn't about shit! I should've listened! You're a sorry ass muthafucka and I hope you get yours. I hope you get everything that's coming to you! You dirty bastard!" Vicki ends the call before Harold can respond. He expected it to go sour. It's not the first time he has had to do it, but he wants to make sure it will be his last. He takes the prepaid phone and hurls it across the room. It hits the wall and shatters. Just as he promised Amanda, he is done.

Harold arrives home from work. He steps into the house expecting his little angel to come running, but gets a hard slap to the face instead. He recoils from the impact. It completely catches him off guard "WHAT THE FUCK!" He yells as he rubs the side of his stinging face. Denise stands before him. Her eyes are blood shot red. She reeks of alcohol and smoke. Her light brunette tendrils are a disheveled mess.

"So you couldn't be man enough to tell me? You had to string me along and waste my time, waste years of my precious life! Why weren't you man enough to do the right thing?"

"What the hell are you talking about?"

"You know exactly what I'm talking about, the young black girl and Carl's wife! That's what the fuck I'm talking about!" Denise's searing words leave Harold speechless. He wonders how she found out about Amanda and Vicki. He also wonders if she has found out about any of his other past flings.

"Whoa, calm down. It's definitely not what you think—"

"Well, you know what I think; I think that you're a lying worthless piece of shit that deserves to never see MY DAUGHTERS AGAIN!"

"Hold on one fucking minute, they're my girls too! You can't keep me away from them and—"

"LIKE HELL I CAN'T! ONCE THE COURT SEES ALL OF YOUR EXTRAMARITAL ACTIVITES, I'M PRETTY SURE THAT THEY WILL AGREE WITH MY DECISION!" Denise's words instantly make Harold think back to his weird meeting earlier.

"That motherfucker was filming me!" He mumbles as he mentally connects the pieces of the puzzle. He knows that he has royally fucked up. He tries to think of something to say that will neutralize the situation, but his mind draws a blank.

"I know about everything, so you need to finally man up and accept the consequences of your actions. I'm done. See you in court!" Denise walks out of the house and leaves Harold alone to stew in his own misery.

After sulking for a few, he decides to call Amanda. "Hey Amanda,"

"Harold? Why are you calling me from a different number? I've been calling your phone like crazy and it kept going to voicemail."

"I got rid of it, it's done. I'm ready to start our new life."

"So you broke it off with your fling and you told Denise?"

"Yes it's all out in the open, no more sneaking around and no more lies. Look, I really need to see you, are you still at Alicia's?"

"Yes but I don't think it would be a good I idea for you to come over here. Carl came by earlier and we had to call to police. He's really out of it. I don't feel safe anymore."

"Okay, so what do you propose we do? It's definitely not a good idea for you to come here."

"How about we meet at that Super Eight?"

"Well actually, I've got a better place in mind."

Amanda pulls up to The Ritz Carlton. She smiles as she thinks about seeing Harold. She is so preoccupied with seeing her love that she fails to notice Carl's car slowly creep from around the corner. He watches as his wife goes inside of the swanky hotel. Amanda is bursting with excitement as she makes her way inside. Harold is all hers. They are officially a couple. She gushes with joy as she steps onto the elevator. She envisions them spending future days together. She reminisces about being in his strong toned arms. She fantasizes about staring into his striking, breathtaking eyes. She throbs as she thinks about his love going inside of her. She feels bad for Denise, but is relieved that after this night, they will no longer have to sneak around. Once she reaches her floor, Amanda calls Harold. "Hi baby, I'm here."

"Okay honey I'm waiting for you." Harold responds as he rises from off of the bed. He is surprised that he managed to dose off without being aware of it. He grabs a mint from off of the nightstand and pops it into his mouth to chase away the odor of sleep. Before Amanda can knock, Harold opens the door. "I missed you," he says before grabbing his woman and giving her a strong passionate kiss. Amanda melts in his strong embrace. She's been waiting all day for this moment. They quickly remove their clothing, and engage. Harold penetrates Amanda's throbbing moist womanhood and she purposely digs her nails into his back. She has wanted to do it for so long and now she is taking full advantage of their exclusivity. She claws and bites his flesh in approval of his sexual labor and for the first time, they make guiltless love. They are free from everything and free to give their all to one another. They engage in one of the rawest, most unadulterated forms of sex. Their sex is explosively primal. Every thrust, every moan, every scratch, every bite is uninhibited. Amanda melts in love as Harold thrusts his frustrations away. They continue to go at it as time slips by, as evening gives way to the night.

Now lying in the Aftermath of hot fulfilling intercourse, they stare into one another's eyes. They communicate without words. Harold and Amanda are completely satisfied. After some time, Harold interrupts their silent communication with a soft sincere declaration. "I want this feeling forever…I want you forever."

DAY 5

9:02am: Harold wakes up with Amanda nestled close to him. Her warm body feels perfect up against his naked flesh. His nose takes in her sweet womanly fragrance as he glances at the rays of sunlight touching her soft exposed skin. He thinks about their future together. In spite of their obstacles with Carl and Denise, he looks forward to making a life with her. He knows that Denise is going to give him hell, but does not quite know what trouble Carl is capable of causing.

He feels terrible about the way things went with Denise. He wishes things would have went differently with her. She deserved better. He knows that if not for her seeing evidence of his infidelity, things would have definitely went better. If his hand had not been forced, he could have easy defused the hostility. He would have handled it by doing what he has always done in those instances. He would have smooth talked her into a calm docile state and then broke the news in a civil manner. He contemplates hiring a full time person to oversee his company's day-to-day operations and devoting more time to his personal life. He knows that with his imminent divorce on the horizon, he is going to have to keep it running smoothly so he can afford to pay lawyer fees, child support, and in a worst case scenario alimony. Seeing as how a sizable amount of his time and attention will be devoted to the messy debacles of divorce and custody cases, he is definitely going to need someone else's clear mind to oversee it.

He shifts his attention back to the object of his affection. Amanda is everything that he has ever wanted in a woman. For the first time in his life, he feels completely satisfied. "Sorry Carl," He mumbles as he thinks about his victory. He feels bad considering how close they once were, but it is hard to have control over whom you fall in love with. If there is a God somewhere, Harold knows that the omnipresent entity is probably not too pleased with him. "Wake up sleepy head," Harold mumbles as he gently strokes Amanda's hair. She rouses and is delighted to find herself next to him

"Hey Papi, mmm last night was great." She murmurs before getting a brief stretch in. "You always know how to please me."

"I wouldn't be your man if didn't. I don't mean to put a damper on the mood that you're in but I would really like to know what happen with Carl yesterday."

"It's cool. As good I'm feeling right now, it'll take a lot more than that to get me down. Anyway, he pulled up outside of Alicia's house with his radio blasting the same song repeatedly it was creepy. He got out of the car and just stood there staring at me. I couldn't tell if he was drunk or high but I knew that something wasn't right about him. I looked up the song afterwards. The song is "Never Gonna Give You Up" by some old soul singer named Jerry "The Iceman" Butler."

"Oh wow really?" Harold blurts as he listens to her story.

"Yeah and up to that point, I had never heard that song before. I wanted to confront him and get him to stop playing that creepy song but I was terrified of him!"

"So how did the cops get involved? I mean what else did he do other than play his music loudly?"

"He didn't do anything else but after hearing the song for a fifth time, Alicia couldn't take it anymore. She's the one that ended up calling the cops. She started yelling at him, telling him that the cops were on their way and if he knew what was good for him, he would leave! After playing the song two more times, he slowly got back in the car and left. It was disturbing. I think he's gone off the deep end. I'm having second thoughts about getting my things from the house. I might need a police escort!"

"Don't worry babes. If worse comes to worse I'll hire some movers and personally see to it that nothing happens to you or your belongings.

"Thanks honey,"

"You're welcome, so have you been looking at some places for us?"

"Yeah, I found a few I liked. I scheduled some appointments

for next week."

"Okay good well enough with all of this seriousness, how about we get a quickie in before checkout time?"

"You read my mind stallion," Amanda responds as she grabs his semi-erect cock. The two begin to kiss and grope in between the soft high thread count, Egyptian cotton sheets. Amanda scoots down and begins servicing Harold. He watches as the sheet covering her head goes up and down over his now erect manhood. Her warm wet mouth deeply engulfs him. He lets out a low manly groan as she passionately blows his mind with her oral precision. Once she is done, she positions herself on top of him. Harold's hard penis plunges into her wetness. She moans as it penetrates her. She begins rhythmically riding his firm pleasure stick. Harold grabs her curves as her walls stroke his stiff penis. He likes to be in control, so he smoothly flips her over and takes charge. He slowly grinds her insides as he kisses her neck. She loves the way his lips feel as they press up against her soft golden skin. Their romp extends past the quickie limit and crosses over into a full session. Hot sex has just turned into full on lovemaking. Harold continues pumping her soft box until she climatically releases in a violent explosion of seizure-like proportions. Harold, so caught up in the moment releases his hot fluid inside of her. They are completely enamored with each other.

"Oh fuck baby! That was incredible!" She exclaims while still shaking.

"Yeah it's always great between us. I'm about to hop in the

shower. Why don't you come and join me."

"Okay as soon as I stop shaking." She shoots back. Harold smiles in approval. He grabs his things and heads into the bathroom. After a few moments of rest, Amanda regains her composure and begins to gather all of her belongings. While gathering her things, a strong feeling of trepidation overtakes her. It is a very intense feeling, unlike anything she has ever experienced before. The feeling is very negative, devoid of hope. She struggles to shake it off but it refuses to leave. She makes it into the bathroom with Harold and it becomes more pronounced. "Hey baby I'm coming in." Amanda says in a forced bubbly tone as she places her stuff on the bathroom counter. She steps into the warm steamy shower. Harold turns to face her. He has a somewhat grim expression.

Unbeknownst to Amanda, Harold has an uneasy feeling as well. He wonders if his guilt is getting the best of him or if it's just a reaction to being under stress.

"Is everything alright?" They ask each other in unison. It freaks them both out. They laugh and try to ignore the feelings. The laughter helps to reduce the bad vibes. In slightly better spirits, the two kiss and caress each other briefly before Harold gets out and Amanda starts to wash up. Once dressed, Harold answers a call from his office. As he finishes his call, Amanda emerges from the bathroom.

"Hey baby, I really have to get out of here. I have to handle a few things at the office." Harold states before grabbing his things and giving her a quick peck. Amanda dries off and follows suit.

As she steps in the elevator, the dreadful sensation resumes. She tries to rationalize the cause of it. She mentally goes over all of the less than great things going on in her life. The only thing that really sticks out is Carl. Her mind stays fixated on him as she reaches the lobby.

Once she gets outside, something else steals her attention. A quick glance at her car has revealed a new addition. There is something stuck underneath one of her windshield wipers. At first, she mistakes it for a parking ticket but as she gets closer, she realizes that it is an envelope. She quickly scans the area as she grabs it from off the windshield. She gets in the car, opens the envelope, and gasps as she views the contents. The contents are pictures of her and Harold! She sees Harold start to pull off and tries frantically to get his attention. Her attempts are unsuccessful. She calls his phone and it goes straight to voicemail. She calls it several more times but to no avail. She immediately starts up her car and tries to catch up with him. She manages to get within a few cars distance. She tries one last time to reach him by phone. Again, it goes to voicemail. "Harold baby, I need you to call me back right away!" She blurts into the phone as panic sweeps over her.

Thinking about Amanda, Harold grabs his phone from out of his pocket. He tries to use it but is unsuccessful. The battery has died. "Damn," he mumbles as he takes out his car charger. He plugs it up and focuses back on the road. Preoccupied with a reckless driver in front of him, he fails to notice Amanda's vehicle five cars behind. He makes the corner just as the light turns red. Leaving Amanda and the rest of the vehicles stuck at the light.

As he is driving, Harold realizes that he forgot some paperwork at the house. He decides to make a quick stop home before heading into the office.

11:32am: Harold arrives at his office. He pulls into the parking garage. He notices Amanda's car parked in his reserved parking spot with the driver side door slightly ajar. "What the fuck?" He questions as he stops in front of it. He gets out of the car and hears an old RnB song emanating from inside of her vehicle. It instantly makes him recall the situation that she told him about earlier. "Never gonna give you up..." He mumbles along with the soul singer as he walks toward her car. As he gets closer, he sees someone is sitting in the driver's seat. He reaches the driver's side and sees Amanda's bloody lifeless body. Her throat has a large slash from ear to ear and the handle of a knife is protruding from her gaped open mouth. "Oh sh—" before Harold can finish his thought, the sound of a gunshot echoes through the garage. Subsequently after, Harold feels a sharp sting in his lower abdomen. He looks down and sees a hole with crimson liquid oozing out of it. He instantly goes into shock.

He turns and sees Carl walking toward him with a smoking gun aimed in his direction. Harold feels his bladder emptying its urine contents as Carl fire two more shots at point blank range.

Both shots hit Harold in the Chest. He falls backwards onto the floor of the garage. He feels a massive pain in his chest as he begins to shake uncontrollably. He starts to get dizzy. He manages to focus his vision and sees Carl standing over him.

"You just had to ruin my life huh? You just had to take everything from me! You couldn't be happy with your family and all of your money! You just had to have her! How could do this to me, twice! I should've known it was you the first time! I should've known that it wasn't one of your employees. The coincidence hit too close to home! You were supposed to be my family! I loved you!" Tears run from Carl's eyes as he stands over his bleeding cousin, childhood memories of them playing together, flash in his head as he looks down at Harold. The memories make Carl's burning rage slowly dissipate, and become replaced by a deep sadness. "You knew how much I loved her, you heartless son of a bitch! I hope it was worth it! I'll see you in hell!" Carl puts the barrel of the gun in his mouth and pulls the trigger.

Harold's ears ring as he fights to hold on. He feels the hot wet blood pooling beneath him. He hears footsteps approaching. "Oh my God," a voice says as the footfalls get closer. Harold feels himself slipping away. He fights to keep conscious but the pain and shock is overwhelmingly real. His chest burns from the bullet wounds. He thinks about Amanda and Carl. He tries to wrap his head around the cold reality that has just forced its way into his crumpling life.

"She's dead…" is the only thought he can process through the

incredible pain ravaging his blood soaked body. He struggles to breath. He feels blood filling into his wounded right lung. He yearns to submit to the comfort of death. He aches to surrender to the inevitable. He wants so desperately to give in and right as he is on the cusp of defeat, he thinks about them... his precious girls. They give him a reason to live, a reason to fight for each short troubled breath. His vision becomes blurry. He tries focusing but to no avail.

"Please God, don't let die," he cries in a garbled tone.

11:43am An Ambulance with a police escort arrives. The Paramedics waste no time getting out. "Where are they at?" one of them asks the garage attendant while the other unloads their equipment.

"They're right over here." The man responds before rushing over towards Harold. "I got a page from upstairs. They said I had a package waiting for me. I got the package, stopped to use the John, and headed back down. When I came back, I saw these people on the ground and I think there's another person in the car." The garage attendant says in an excited manner.

"Okay, well do you know these people?" The paramedic questions as he helps prepare the stretcher.

"He's the owner," he points to Harold, "I don't know the other guy or the person in the car. I think it's a lady."

"I'm about to patch for backup," the paramedic says before radioing in "This is Randall Jones, 10-88. We need more paramedics. We got an LOC possibly two and another one critically wounded..." Randall's voice trails off as Harold begins to fade.

"Stay with me!" Randall's partner Jason instructs as he frantically works to keep Harold among the living. Harold comes back briefly but fades again. He is on the brink of death. Randall and Jason get Harold in the Ambulance just as more assistance is arriving. Randall briefs the other EMTs before heading off with sirens blaring and lights flashing. "C'mon man, don't slip on me, hang in there!" Jason pleads as the Ambulance hustles through traffic.

"Oh lord..." Harold says before his eyes roll. He feels his soul separating from his wounded flesh. A single tear drops from his eye as he takes his last breath.

Chrome Justice

1
RAIN

He stands emotionless. Numb from the bloodshed; detached from the world around him, soaked in rain mixed with blood. His handgun loosely clutched in his hand, a knife cradled in the other. The hard rainfall and flashing red & blue lights do little to break his state of shock. The shouting voices of the police officers sound like they are a million miles away. Sean is unfazed by all of it. He knew it might end like this. He did what he had to do. They had to pay for what they took away from him. They paid for his loss with their blood. He knows what he did tonight won't bring her back, but it will help bring closure.

He knows it is over. He is relieved, even though he knows he is fucked at the same time. He drops his weapons and slowly raises his hands as federal agents and local police converge on him. The first officer in forcefully snatches Sean's right arm out of the air. He feels the cold metal close in around his wrist as the other arm is forced to follow suit. The agent begins stating his Miranda rights to him. "You have the right to remain silent…"

"Yeah, yeah, yeah," Sean thinks to himself as they barbarically man handle him towards the patrol car. They spare no expense on force as they shove him in the back seat. They barely give him enough time to get his last leg in before slamming the door behind him. "Fucking Assholes" Sean mumbles while giving them the most evil facial expression that the muscles in his face will allow. *"The reason why I'm here is because these Fuckers can't do their jobs!"* he thinks while looking at the cops from out of the squad car window. After what seems like an eternity of waiting, two cops finally get into the front of the vehicle. The one on the passenger side turns to face Sean.

"Hello Mr. Vigilante." He says sarcastically while sneering. The ride to the station is long and riddled with taunts and insults from the cop in the passenger seat. Once they get to their destination, Sean is booked; finger printed, stripped of his personal belongings, and placed in a holding cell.

"Detective Warren will see you when he arrives." The officer says before closing the cell door. Sean is extremely tired. His body and mind are equally drained. He settles onto the hard jail cot and waits for sleep to overtake him.

"WAKE UP MR. WEST!" A large voice booms from outside of the cell. It grabs Sean from out of his slumber and slams him back into his haphazard reality. He can hear keys jangling on the other side of the door. The guard opens the door as Sean stands to his feet. The guard places handcuffs on him, though not as rough as the police officer that arrested him. Once cuffed, the guard leads escorts Sean into a small room down the hall from the cell. "Have a seat, the detective will be in shortly," The guard says while removing the cuffs. He exits the room and leaves Sean alone to his thoughts. Sean looks around the room. The room has a double-sided mirror that covers almost all of one complete wall. It also has a surveillance camera in the upper left corner. The room is sparsely furnished. A worn beaten table sits in the middle of it accompanied by two hard wooden chairs. Sean seats himself in one of them. He notices a lone coffee mug with stale coffee and a dirty cheap ashtray littered with butts and ash resting on the table. The sight of the coffee mug with cold coffee and the ashtray with cigarette remnants triggers recently repressed urges in Sean. He finds himself seriously jonesing for both a nicotine and caffeine fix. The door handle begins to twist. The door opens. A man enters the room. His hard-nosed looks make it quite clear what his profession is. He has dark brown skin that is a sharp contrast to his starch white shirt. He looks long and hard at Sean. He has a piercing stare that can intimidate even the most hardened criminal. His penchant for justice is evident in his mannerisms. He has a manila folder with papers inside of it. He places the folder on the table, takes off his suit coat, and rests it on the chair opposite of Sean.

"Mr. West I am Detective Warren," the man says in a deep richly intimidating tone. "I am going to ask you a series of questions and I'm expecting to get answers to them all." He says while removing his hat and picking up the folder. Sean West sits quietly. His mixed heritage is quite apparent in his features. His dark curly short but wild hair and scruffy beard give him the look of a desperado. His hazel eyes are filled with deep sadness and remorse. His bloody tattered clothing looks like it is fresh off Hell's fashion rack. He sits on the wooden uncomfortably hard chair while Detective Warren paces around the room.

"Excuse me Detective Warren can I get a cup of coffee and a cigarette?" Sean asks. Detective Warren walks over to the two sided mirror and taps on it.

"Yes Mr. Warren?" a voice says over the intercom.

"Hey Mac, give me some smokes and coffee." Detective Warren responds.

"Right away sir," the voice through the intercom says. Detective Warren takes a long hard look at Sean before speaking.

"Sean I need you to be completely honest with me." Detective Warren says while fumbling through the manila folder. He pulls out a picture and shows it to Sean. "Do you know this man?" Sean looks at the picture. He recognizes the man but plays dumb.

"No I've never seen him before." Detective Warren gives a slight giggle before going into beast mode.

"YOU'RE A FUCKING LIAR SEAN!" He says before slapping the ashtray across the room.

He circles him like a shark circling wounded prey. In a fit of frustration, Detective Warren grabs Sean and partially yanks him out of the chair. "What the fuck is your problem? You think just because you have a gun you can go out and be a fucking vigilante?" Detective Warren asks while shaking Sean West like a crazed parent. "Just because you have a gun and a vendetta doesn't mean put your life at risk or those of innocent bystanders! Thanks to your performance earlier we have a 12 year old barely clinging to life after being hit with two stray bullets! Don't get me wrong those cancers deserved every fucking thing that came to them! They have been a thorn in this precinct's side for the longest!" Detective Warren backs off and collects himself. His words are like bullets ripping through Sean's soul.

"Damn a 12 year old got shot! I didn't mean for things to end how they did but they had to die!" Sean thinks to himself as he tries to sort out his emotions. "Look Mr. Warren, you don't know what it's like to lose a wife. Rebecca was everything to me! She isn't here because of them! I wish the child didn't get hurt I really do but they had it coming. They had to pay...THEY HAD TO DIE!"

"I understand how you feel Sean, I really do, but we need to do our job. An innocent child is the victim just like your wife was so we need to bring justice to him and his family as well. Now if you cooperate, we can get you a deal. I will personally make sure of it. We can play the angle of self-defense and ensure that you go into a minimum-security mental facility for a few years. It will be under the guise that you are receiving rehabilitation for mental anguish and post traumatic stress after the loss of your wife. Do you follow what I'm saying? We will spin it so that in the judge and/or juries' eyes you will be a victim that had no choice but to fight back. In spite of everything, you need to have a fresh start on life. You deserve to go back to living as much of a normal life as possible."

Sean sits and thinks about the deal that the Detective has just presented to him. *"The Detective is right. I deserve the right to try to pick up the pieces. I have avenged Rebecca, she would want me to."* He thinks before speaking. The door opens and a man enters the room with cigarettes and coffee.

"Thanks Mac." Detective Warren says.

"You're welcome," the man says before leaving back out of the room. Detective Warren pours coffee into a mug and places it in front of Sean along with sugar packets, a spoon, a lighter, and the pack of cigarettes. Sean puts the sugar in his coffee and lights a cigarette. He takes a long drag before speaking.

"He was there. The man in the picture was there. He was the one that helped me. He never told me his name." Sean looks down and searches for the right words to say. "There was something very different about him...he didn't seem...all the way there...it was like...he was a shell of a man. When I asked him his name, he referred to himself as THE HUNTER."

2
ALL FALLS DOWN

The streets of Garland, Ohio are in great unrest. Tax-paying citizens live in fear. They are prisoners to the city's criminal element. A war for control is raging. The Sin Lords and the Blood Money Family are embroiled in a bitter battle. Territorial pushbacks are the norm and murder is just another commonplace occurrence. Casualties are being racked up on both sides. Innocent bystanders have fallen victim to the carnage. Robert Cross aka The Lord, leader of the Sin Lords (SL for short), has vowed to take over the streets. His archrival James Johnson aka Blood, is the founder of the Blood Money Family also known as BMF.

At this very moment, a shoot-out is taking place between several members of the SL and the BMF. Two vehicles are racing through the streets. BMF members Change, Redd, Jay Blood, and Lance are in a black late model SUV pursuing a dark blue Chevy Sedan containing Sin Lords members Butch, Vig, Rico, and Wallace.

"Man we need to hurry up and lose these Muthafuckas!" Rico says as he reloads his gun. He is a Puerto Rican man in his early twenties with a long bushy ponytail and dark eyes. A bullet shatters the back window and rips through Rico's throat. Blood splatters across the back of the driver's seat. Rico instinctively grabs his neck and panics. He tries to scream but the blood in his throat drowns out the sound. He manages to let out a few gurgles before passing out.

"Fuck this shit! Butch, slow this Muthafucka down. I'm bout to take these Bitches out!" With that being said, Wallace a white male in his mid-twenties hangs out the window and fires his Uzi. The bullets make contact with the front tire, the windshield, and the head of a brown-skinned black man named Change, the driver of the SUV. Another bullet nearly misses Redd's left shoulder, tears through his seat, and rips into Lance's chest. The young black male instinctively grabs his chest and moans in agony as the pain from the wound intensifies.

"Oh shit you got them bitches. Let's get the fuck out of here!" Vig the heavyset Hersey colored man says as the Chevy u-turns and speeds off in the opposite direction. The SUV continues hurling down the street swerving as Redd, a light-skinned twenty something black male tries to move Change's lifeless body out of the way and get control of the vehicle.

"Come on man we gotta kick this nigga outta the car!" Jay Blood says as he reaches out of the backseat passenger window and frantically tries to grab the driver side door handle. The dreaded young thug has had many close calls but this one may surpass them all.

"But that's Change!" Redd protests, the hue of his freckle littered face matching his nickname.

"Look that nigga dead, and we gonna end up the same way unless you do what I say!" Jay snaps. "When I get this shit open, push his ass out!" he commands as Redd nods in agreement. Jay manages to get a grip on the handle. He tugs at it but the door won't budge. "Hurry up and get that shit open!" Jay yells in a panicked voice as Red pushes on the door from the inside.

Rebecca, a Hispanic/White woman in her mid-thirties is full of joy. Her dark brown hair is neatly bunched up in a ponytail. Her full face glows with enthusiasm. Her warm bright eyes are filled with a deep love for life. After years of trying to conceive, her and her husband's prayers have finally been answered. Filled with the spirit of motherhood, she sees a baby boutique on the way to her appointment and cannot resist stopping in. She figures she might as well check it out since she has forty-five minutes until her Doctor's appointment. She estimates that she has at least fifteen minutes to spare. With her car parked, she wastes no time going in.

Once inside the store, she practically begins picking up everything blue and for a boy. She pictures her future son in every outfit she pulls off a rack. She imagines him taking his first steps, making his first mess, saying his first words. After having waited for what seemed like an eternity to conceive, the fact that she isn't getting what she really wanted, a pretty in pink girl doesn't matter the least. The most important thing to Rebecca now is that she is going to be a Mom.

Rebecca looks at her phone to check the time. The time is fifteen after one. Her appointment is set for one-forty-five. Not wanting to chance being late, she starts making her way to the checkout. When she gets to the checkout, the cashier greets her in a friendly manner. Rebecca does the same. The cashier quickly rings up all of the items.

"Your total is $47.85," the cashier says after totaling the items.

"Okay," Rebecca responds while rummaging through her purse in search of her wallet. She locates her wallet and takes it out. She flips it open. A picture of a man makes her smile. She stops and looks at the wedding band on her finger. After a moment of reflection, she locates her bankcard and pulls it out.

"Can I use this card?"

"Yes you can," the cashier responds.

After paying for her items, Rebecca leaves the store. *"Mmm I probably should've got that other outfit. That color blue is so cute!"* She thinks as she starts to walk to her car. At that moment, she notices a black vehicle headed towards her. "Oh Sh—" Before she can finish her thought, the SUV Slams into her. She barely misses being smashed into a pole by mere inches. The force of the impact sends her flying through the air. She bounces off a parked car and hits the ground with a hard thud. The way she lands, forces her body into an unnatural position. She feels intense pain as part of her spinal column breaks.

Sean West is just getting ready to take a late lunch when his office phone begins to ring.

"Mr. West?"

"Yes Melissa?"

"Sir you have an urgent call on the line. I'm about to transfer it to you right now."

"Okay, thank you." The call transfers

"Hello Mr. West?"

"Yes this is he."

"Mr. West This is Susan from South Point Hospital. There has been an accident...we need you to come down to the hospital right away...it's your wife Rebecca."

"What's the problem? Is there complications with the pregnancy?"

"Uh, no sir... she... was in a car accident today."

"What! Is she—" Before Sean can finish, Susan interrupts.

"No but—" Now Sean interrupts Susan.

"I'm coming right now!" He says before hanging up. He gathers his things and rushes out of his office. He sees Melissa on his way out "Melissa, please tell Mr. Washington that I'm leaving. It's a family emergency!"

"Ok Mr. West," Melissa responds before Sean rushes out of the door.

Sean makes his way to the garage and gets in his car. He starts it up. His heart pounds as his thoughts race. He swipes his card at the gate and barely gives the gate arm time to lift up. The car zooms through the streets. Sean tries his best to do the speed limit but his foot feels like it's full of lead. His nerves are all over the place. He reaches into his armrest and pulls out a pack of cigarettes. "I know I promised Rebecca I was going to quit but I really need this right now." He says to himself as he pushes in the car lighter. He lights the cigarette and takes several puffs. After a few minutes, a slight calm sweeps over him. His mind rewinds back to the morning. He remembers waking up next to Rebecca. His mind flashes forward to their last kiss and him rubbing her baby bump before leaving for work.

He manages to make it to the Hospital in less than fifteen minutes. He recklessly parks in the first available spot he can find. He doesn't know what to expect as gets out of the car. *"How bad is she? Is she going to make it? How is the baby? Is he okay?"* These thoughts manifest in his head as he makes his way into the hospital. Once inside, he heads directly to the help desk. "Hi can you please tell me where I can find the patient Rebecca West?"

"Hello sir, give me a second while I look her up." The person behind the service desk responds. "According to our system, she is still in Intensive Care."

"Intensive Care," Sean exclaims as an intense rush of dread sweeps over him.

"Yes sir Intensive Care. If you take that hallway," she points in the direction as she talks "all the way down to the end and turn left, it will take you right there."

"Thank You," Sean says before racing down the hall. He reaches the nurse desk and wastes no time asking about Rebecca. "Hi, I'm Sean West and I'm looking for my wife Rebecca West."

"Mrs. West is still in surgery."

"Is she going to make it?" Sean asks as he forces back the tears fighting to be released from his eyes.

"It looks very hopeful." The nurse's response helps to put Sean's most dreaded fear to rest.

"Thank God, when will I be able to see her?"

"I'm not quite sure at the moment but if you sign in and wait in the waiting area, I will personally make sure that you see her as soon as she is out of surgery."

"Okay," Sean responds, "Is it okay if I step outside and have a quick smoke?

"Yes as long as you go to the designated area across the street off of the premises."

"Okay." Sean says before going outside.

Sean smokes his cigarette while trying to push all of the negative thoughts out of his head. In spite of his shaking hands and troubled short breaths, he manages to get some level of calm from his nicotine fix. He finishes his cigarette and goes back into the hospital. As sits and waits, he feels himself starting to relax. It's been a long trying day. He takes out his cell phone and checks for missed calls. The phone doesn't show any missed calls. He then opens up a game and begins playing it. He plays it until he starts feeling drowsy. After a while of playing, he puts it up and starts focusing on the television that's on in the room. There is a news program on. He recognizes the newscaster. Her name is Camilla Stevens. Sean went to school with her older brother all the way up until the eighth grade.

"This Is Camilla Stevens reporting live at the scene of a thwarted robbery attempt. Earlier today, two armed gunmen forced their way into a local credit union as it was closing for the day demanding money. Eye witnesses say that this man" (A picture of a black man in his mid-30's flashes on the screen.) *"Single handedly stopped them as they were exiting the building. According the witness statements, the mystery man came out of nowhere firing shots at the gunmen. Both men sustained injuries but are expected to recover. We have one of the witnesses here live. Mr. Williams a neighbor of the credit union says he witnessed the entire event."*

"Those guys got what they deserved! The one fella appeared outta nowhere like Batman or the Punisher. They tried to shoot him but he was quicker on the draw. Once he put those scumbags outta commission, he disappeared as quick he appeared. The Police department needs to offer him a job!"

"Thank you Mr. Williams, police are offering an award for any information in regards to this case. This is Camilla Stevens for 5-action news."

"Wow we have a vigilante in the city." Sean thinks as the news segment goes off. He continues to watch the television until he slowly drifts off to sleep.

3
DOWN BUT NOT OUT

SEAN IS STANDING in the middle of fog. He looks in every direction and sees nothing but more fog. He hears sounds in one direction and starts running towards them. The sounds get clearer the closer he gets to them. He now recognizes them as gunfire. He gets even closer and they change from gunfire to church bells. The fog starts to clear away and he sees a church. He notices people going inside. The people are all dressed in black and have somber facial expressions. He follows them into the church and it dawns on him that they are attending someone's funeral. The people going inside pay little attention to Sean as he falls into the crowd going in.

Once inside, a woman lying in a casket catches his attention. She looks familiar. He proceeds up to the casket. The woman starts to get more recognizable as he draws nearer to it. He finally reaches the casket and is shocked by the person resting in it. The woman in the casket is Rebecca! She opens her eyes and slow rises from out of it. Her face is pale and devoid of life. Her eyes are milky white. Once risen, she opens her mouth and starts calling Sean.

"Mr. West. Mr. West. Mr.—" Sean awakens to a medical staff member standing over him. "Mr. West you can come back now and see Rebecca." the staff member says as Sean tries to shake the heavy slumber off.

"How long was I sleep?" He wonders as he searches for his phone. He checks the time and notices it's the next morning. He gets up and follows the staff member back to Rebecca's room. He enters the room and sees his wife Rebecca sound asleep. She looks peaceful as she sleeps in spite of the fact that she has several different wires and cords attached to her. Sean takes a seat next to her, grabs her hand, and begins to cry. It starts out as a small whimper then, it explodes from out of him in a rush of wet emotion. He tries to contain it but it's too much to get a handle on. *"Thank God it was only a dream!"* He thinks as he continues to hold her hand. He strokes her hair with his other hand. He can't wait for her to awaken. He wonders how things will be when she does. He wonders about the baby. *"Did he make it? And if he did, will he be okay when he comes out?"* He feels angry just thinking about the possibility of the baby not surviving. His cell phone begins vibrating in his pocket. Sean takes it out and looks at the screen. It's his father. He answers the phone.

"Hey Dad,"

"Hello Sean, how is Rebecca doing?"

"Well right now she is asleep. She just came out of surgery."

"Good. Thank God, she's alive. How are you doing? How is the baby? I called your office and they told me what happened."

"I'm okay, the baby…well I'm not sure right now."

"Oh okay… well, keep me posted. I will tell Lin as well."

"Alright dad, tell her to give me a call."

"I will."

"Let me call you back in a few Pops."

"Okay Sean." Sean ends the call. His focus shifts back on Rebecca. His emotions are mixed between sadness and anger. *"How could this happen? How could something so horrible happen to a person so good?"* While Sean is in the middle of his thoughts, there is a knock at the door.

"Come in," Sean says. Two men in suits enter the room.

"Hello Sir. You must be Mr. West, I'm detective Bradley, and this is my partner detective Spurlock." One of the men says before pulling out a business card. "We're the officers assigned to your wife's case." He hands Sean the business card. "We stopped by to see if your wife was able to answer a few questions but I see now isn't a good time. Here's my card. We will be in touch." Sean examines the card

"Okay thanks," he says as the men prepare to leave back out of the room. "Wait before you leave…can you tell me exactly what happened?"

"Well according to our records, your wife was struck by an out of control vehicle as she was leaving a baby boutique on Western Avenue yesterday afternoon."

"What was wrong with the driver? Was he under the influence?"

"No. Actually...he was dead, a victim of gunshots. We believe it may have been gang related. We have a few leads right now. Contact us as soon as Rebecca is ready. Try to have good evening Mr. West." The men begin to exit the room. As they are leaving, Sean's phone begins to vibrate. He answers it. It is Rebecca's best friend. They exchange pleasantries and she informs him that she will make it into town as soon as possible. As Sean finishes his conversation, he hears a beep indicating another incoming call. He finishes the call and switches lines.

"Hello,"

"Hey big bro how is everything. Is Rebecca okay?"

"Yes for the most part..." Sean pauses to try to contain his emotions but it is of no use, everything floods out. He feels the warm wet trickles of tears roll down both sides of his face. He tries his best to keep the tremble in his voice under control before continuing to speak. "I don't know if she still has the baby and I don't know how Rebecca is doing because she is still sleep."

"Awww she's going to be okay. What happened to her?"

"Well I don't know exactly. She got out of surgery a few hours ago. Some Detectives just left as well. They informed me that she was struck by an out of control vehicle as she was leaving a baby boutique."

"Oh my God...I'm on my way which hospital are you at?"

"We're at South Point Hospital."

"Okay I'll be there in a few,"

"Okay," Sean gets off the phone with Linda and turns his focus back to Rebecca. He lays his head on her and begins to cry. He lets it all out. He thinks about the baby and cries even harder. He is uncertain about the future. He can't see anything pass the present. Every fiber of his being is involved in his emotional release. He feels detached from himself. He wrestles with the spirit of negativity. He pushes himself to keep holding on to optimism. After awhile he feels himself drifting off. A knock on the door quickly awakens him. "Come in," Sean says while trying his best to shake off the drowsiness. Sean's sister Linda enters the room. She is a slim, fair-skinned young woman in her late 20's with long hair, and wide captivating gray eyes. She rushes over and gives Sean a hug.

"How are you holding up?" she asks while trying to wipe Sean's face with her saliva dipped fingers.

"Ugh Lin stop, you know I hate that!" Sean says with a semi smile.

"Grandma used to do that to you all the time."

"Yeah I know and I didn't like it when she did it either!"

"So did <u>you know who</u> call you?"

"Who,"

"You know, her,"

"No. You told her didn't you?"

"I didn't tell her. Dad did,"

"Oh, I don't know why he felt the need to tell her!"

"Well you know how dad is. He still has something for her."

"Yeah I know," Sean is amazed at how his father still cares for the woman that left him and their family. "Well if she calls I will tell her exactly how I feel!" Sean feels his blood start to boil as he thinks about the woman that he used to call mother. His disdain for her runs deep. He remembers the day she left as if it were yesterday. He remembers coming home from school and going into his hiding place to find an empty jar! All the money he'd saved for years to help with his college tuition was gone All of the summers spent working while his friends played and enjoyed their youth was all in vain. His mother had taken his savings to buy more drugs. Her drug habit tore their happy home apart. His father tried his best to shield them from their mother's ill ways but even he did not expect her to do what she did. The many nights that Sean would hear his father crying, only added more fuel to the raging inferno. The taunts from the kids at school helped solidify Sean's stance on never forgiving her. "Lin I really don't want that Bitch coming up here or giving me any of her sympathy!"

"Sean you really need to forgive—" before Linda can finish her sentence, Sean interrupts.

"I will never forgive her! Dad had to take out a second mortgage just to help me pay for college! He sat up and cried so many nights that I've lost count! How could she steal almost six grand from her own son? Don't you remember how embarrassed you were when you went downtown to catch a movie with your friends and ended up running into her? You cried to me that whole night and I had to rock you to sleep!" Linda thinks about what Sean has said before speaking.

"Sean all I'm saying is that you need to forgive her for yourself... to help you heal and overcome. I'm not saying for you to act as if it never happened, I'm saying just give yourself closure. If she comes up here, accept her sympathy. She is trying to show you she cares." Linda says while maintaining eye contact with Sean. Linda's eyes make Sean feel bad about being so hard on their mother. Deep down he knows she is right. Nevertheless, something inside won't let him release the bitter emotions that he has held onto for almost twenty years.

"Look Lin, I can't promise anything, but I will try. I will try my best to at least be cordial if and when she comes up here to visit." Sean and Linda hug as they say their goodbyes. Linda leaves as Sean begins to reflect on their conversation. He looks at Rebecca. Something inside overtakes him. He drops to his knees and begins to say a silent prayer. "Lord, please forgive me and help heal my heart. And please let Rebecca make it." He finishes his prayer and tries desperately to stay awake just in case Rebecca awakens. He doesn't want to miss anything. He feels the need for a cigarette growing from within. He knows that smoking them will only help in the now and do more harm in the end. He steps out of the room and makes the long journey back out to appease his inner nicotine junkie.

He reaches the outside and barely makes it to the designated area before lighting up. His emotions are scrambled. He feels numb, numb to everything. Sean feels like the weight of the universe rests on his shoulders. Tears run down his face as he continues to smoke on the menthol cancer stick; relying on it to bring him some sense of comfort. He feels a white-hot anger rising in his soul. The beginning stages of hate are setting in.

4
THE HUNTER

THE HUNTER is quietly perched on the second floor of an old processing plant. Outdated machinery, scattered paper, and debris surround him. The air in the room is stale and filled with the stench of dust and mice feces. He waits quietly, staring intensely at a group of cars pulling into the parking lot of a neighboring abandoned warehouse. He watches a group of men pile out of the vehicles and head toward the building. His anticipation grows as he continues to watch. A few minutes later, more vehicles arrive. He gets even more anxious as the second group goes in. A deal is about to go down. The moment that he has been waiting for is almost at hand. He is hungry for justice, and starving for revenge! If things go down tonight as planned, he will be another step closer to his goal. He will be a little closer to his end game. The trap has already been set. He has been scoping this location out for weeks. This is where the city's largest crime organization engages in illicit business activities. The place where half of the city's "King" drug supply enters. He has to put a stop to it. The cops won't do it. Most of them are on the take. Corruption runs rampant through Garland's law enforcement. The city needs a true enforcer. A real force of justice, Herrick is the man for the job.

As the dealers get into position, Herrick readies his detonation device and begins a quick countdown. As soon as his lips push out the number one, Herrick presses the button. KABOOM, an explosion rocks the entire building and fills it with smoke. Herrick emerges from his perch and rushes toward the neighboring warehouse. Once he reaches the warehouse, he wastes no time going in. He has one thing left to do before his task is complete. He has to finish any survivors. He sees a man scurrying away. POP, POP, he sends two bullets into the frame of the survivor. Blood sprays out of the bullet wounds as the man collapses. He finds another…POP, and sends a bullet into the brain of the hapless victim. Blood and brain matter splatters as the bullet leaves its exit wound. The man hits the ground and flops about like a fish out of water. He clears out the room in less than a minute. He is taking no prisoners, everyone dies; everyone he kills is guilty. He checks to make sure he has eliminated all targets before searching the area for money and drugs. He locates a briefcase full of money and the shipment of drugs. He grabs the briefcase of money, and heads toward the exit.

Once outside, he lights a cigarette and takes a few puffs before removing another detonation device from his leather trench coat. He heads to one of his victims cars. He takes out a can of spray paint and tags his signature onto the hood of the vehicle. He leaves the mark of the HUNTER! He pushes the button on the device while swiftly returning across the street. BOOM, the explosion rocks the entire block. Flames and billows of smoke find their way out of the crumbling, weakened structure of a warehouse. Once inside his car, he places the briefcase in the passenger seat, turns on his police scanner, revs up his dark blue dodge challenger, and peels off into the night. He hears sirens in the distance as he flees. The voice of the dispatcher echoes over the sound of the running motor as Herrick continues towards his next stop. He wants to rest but his determination want let him. He has one last thing to do before retiring for the night. Glimpses of his old life flash in his mind. Ghosts of the past invade his thoughts as he cruises through the sparsely lit streets of the industrial district. These ghosts are what keeps him determined. He fights to purge the demons that are haunting him out of his system. He struggles to keep some trace of humanity. His heart has grown cold. The world has made him this way. The loss of someone near and dear to him in recent years has only made it worse. He can still hear his lost dark angel's voice reverberating in the recesses of his mind. Her essence haunts every facet of his new life. Thoughts of what could've been constantly torment his psyche. The memories fuel his passion for justice, pushes him to go the extra mile to right as many wrongs as possible.

He turns onto a side street in a rough part of town and shuts off his headlights. Even in the darkness, the dilapidated state of the houses on the street is still quite evident. He drives slowly, taking in everything around him. He remembers this neighborhood well. He slows down near an empty field and parks. He cautiously gets out of his vehicle. The last thing he wants to do is alert any potential witnesses. A near death experience has left him with a heightened sixth sense. He feels who he is looking for. He reaches an old ran down single-family house. It stops him dead in his tracks. The sense is unmistakable. He notices a light on in one of the rooms. He slips around to the back of the house. He reaches the back door and begins working on the lock. He is almost done with the lock when. BOOM, buckshot pellets burst through the door. They hit Herrick square in the chest. He stumbles back before falling. The door opens. A stocky man of Hispanic decent emerges from the door with a shotgun in hand. He stands over Herrick examining the damage.

"I figured you would come for me." The man says as he aims the gun at Herrick's head. "I heard the streets talking about you, the Ghost of Garland. I don't know how you survived the setup, but you won't be surviving this." The man says as he aims his shotgun at Herrick. Herrick with unnaturally fast speed pulls out his gun and fires two shots up at the man. The impact of the bullets, cause the man to lose his grip on the shotgun. It falls to the ground along with its owner. Herrick springs onto his feet. He briefly examines his bulletproof vest.

"H-how..." is all that the wounded man can manage to utter.

"Luis you always were a dumb muthafucka. Bullet proof vest Dumbass!" Herrick says in an angry tone as he taps on his chest. "The only thing that did was piss me off! Now if you want to keep what's left of your shitty life, you will call "The Cleanup Squad" and tell them that you have a job!" He demands with the barrel of his gun pointed at Louis.

"Okay, okay...fuck, don't kill me!" Luis says as he frantically removes his cell phone from his pocket. He dials the number and tries to calm himself down as he waits for someone to answer. Finally, someone answers. "I need Sofia to come home now," he says as he tries to remain composed. Herrick keeps the pistol aimed at him, not flinching for a second. He recognizes Luis's code phrase from back when he used to do business with him. As soon as Louis ends the call, Herrick shoves the gun into his face.

"Get up now and start walking into the house!" Herrick demands. Blood leaks from Luis's wounds as he struggles to get off the ground. He looks down at himself. He sees blood seeping through his pants and shirt. He feels the sting of the gunshot wounds in his right thigh and torso. The sight of the blood triggers instant panic.

"Oh fuck." He murmurs as Herrick forces him into the house at gunpoint. Once inside, Herrick hits Luis in the back of the head with the butt of the pistol. The hit renders him unconscious. He pulls out a pair of handcuffs and drags Luis over to a water pipe leading from the basement. He secures Luis and waits for "The

Cleanup Squad" to arrive. Herrick isn't worried about police interference, especially not after a recent scandal involving crooked cops and a drug network, and the fact that most of the residents aren't fond of calling them works in his favor as well. He estimates that he will have enough time to handle "The Cleanup Squad" and make a clean get away. He starts to feel soreness from the impact of the buckshot. Vest or no vest, the shit still hurts! Times like these make him reminisce. They make him relive the night when everything changed, the night when Karma served him a fresh bowl of payback. Idle time forces him to think about his love lost.

When they first met, her looks and dangerous demeanor instantly caught his heart and held it captive. His mind replays their first encounter and brings a smile to his war hardened face. When they met, he was just getting his feet wet in the world of assassination and she was already making a name for herself. Before he became an assassin, he did a stint in the marines. He learned how to kill for his country long before he learned how to kill for profit. She learned the ropes another way. The way that she learned will forever remain a mystery. Herrick loved her, but never really knew her. That's how it often was in their line work.

The sound of a car pulling up abruptly puts an end to Herrick's trip down memory lane. He quickly scurries downstairs. He waits by the back door for the men. Clean up men, never use front doors. He knows that his shots have to be quick and precise. The men that he will be going up against are trained, but not as well as he is. He slows his breathing, and focuses on the sound of their voices and footsteps. He is as calm and still as a corpse on a slab in the morgue. His sixth sense aids him. It allows him to sense the men. It's just as he suspected, it's two of his failed assassins. He knows exactly what he is going to do. He remains dormant until the right moment. As soon as the right moment comes, he goes into action. The sound of the last foot stepping on the landing outside of the door triggers him. He lets off a series of shots through the wooden door. They hit exactly where he intended them to hit. Both men collapse to the ground. Herrick opens the door and moves quickly out of the house. He lays eyes on his prey. The bullets did their job. The shots have left them as vulnerable as newborns on a changing table.

"You thought I wasn't going to come for you huh?" He says as he pulls a Newport from out of his coat. He sparks it up and takes a few puffs.

"You fucking Nigger, you're not gonna get away with this!" One of the injured men yells as he frantically struggles to move. His wounds have left him in a semi-paralytic state. "You fucking monkey, once Vinnie catches you, they're going to hang you like your black ass deserves!" The racial insults don't faze Herrick. He has heard worse. He has been called every name in the book. Nigger, Coon, Jiggaboo, Negroid, Spook, Porch Monkey, he is above all of it. He smirks at the injured racist as he takes a few more drags off the Newport.

"Tell the devil he's on my list too! He says as he pulls a handgun from out of his coat. One shot to the brain, quickly disposes of the racist piece of trash. The remaining injured man keeps silent as he looks up at Herrick. He sweats bullets as he mentally prays to his god. He suddenly remembers lines of prayers from his Catholic past.

"Hey man it was just business and I wasn't the one that pulled the trigger!" The man blurts out as perspiration floods his face.

"I'm not gonna kill you, I need you to deliver a message for me. Tell Cross I'm coming for him!" He says before digging into the man's pocket and pulling out a cell phone. He dials 911 and places it in the man's sweaty blood covered hand. He smiles before putting out his half-smoked cigarette on his victims sweat soaked face. The man lets out a painful scream as the 911 operator answers the line. Herrick pockets the used cigarette and heads to his car. He jumps into his vehicle and begins his trip back to his hideout. The night went as planned. The deeds done tonight will bring Cross back into the streets, back to where he will pay with his blood!

Herrick reaches his hideout before sunrise. It's an old abandoned factory on the Westside of the city. Decades ago, the area was known for its abundance of blue-collar jobs. Many factories thrived here in its heyday. Now the hollowed out shells of manufacturing facilities is all that remains. Herrick has made some major alterations to it to keep him alert at all times. Custom made alarms and traps adorn almost every inch of his lair. He has converted an old cafeteria into a weapons room. The cabinets are filled with nothing but artillery. He keeps only a few edibles in the fridge. Herrick takes off his war torn attire, and goes into a small room adjacent to the kitchen area. Inside the room, a makeshift shower is rerouted from an old sink. Two towels and a washcloth hang from a lone bar next to the shower. A mirror is stationed above the sink. Herrick stares into the mirror. He has changed so much. He doesn't recognize the reflection staring back at him. The spark of life that was once alive and in his eyes has long since died. A cold hard stare is all that remains. His mind never rests. The hunger for revenge and his past are what it stays focused on, he relives his death daily. He remembers each agonizing second of it. The sound of the heart monitor machine flat lining still echoes in his head. He gets chills as he recalls lying on the cold autopsy table in the morgue and coming back to life mere seconds before the first incision. Herrick steps into the shower and turns on the water. The lukewarm water rains down from the showerhead. The temperature of the water has little effect on Herrick. Those sensitivities died when his original life ended. All he feels now is the pain of a broken heart. He rubs the bruise left by the impact of the shotgun blast. As the water heats up, it helps to take the edge off it. He can feel the soreness dissipate as the now hot steamy water massages it. He makes sure not to get too relaxed. A hunter can never let his guard down.

After a quick wash, Herrick exits the shower. He grabs one of the towels from off of the bar and notices something move out of the corner his eye. He turns quickly and notices a mouse scurrying into the wall. Sights like this remind him of just how disgusting his life has become. His whole life is now one big parade of death and mayhem with a little bit of justice thrown into the mix for good measure. Never the less, it will be all worth it in the end. After a few hours of sleep, he will be good as new. The speed at which he heals is slightly above that of a normal human. Herrick attempts to get rest, but his adrenaline is still pumping. He can't wait to get back out on the streets. He has more fish to fry.

Finally able to relax, Herrick slowly drifts off. His mind soon begins to replay one of its many hellish flashback sequences. He opens his eyes to total darkness. He hears many familiar voices coming from all directions. A small light in the distance interrupts the darkness. Herrick feels his body moving towards the light. The light gets brighter and more distinguished as he gets closer. He gets close enough to see that the light is coming from a room with its door slightly ajar. The voices are coming from inside of it. They are distinctly clear now. It sounds like two people arguing. He is on the verge of walking in the door when a loud buzz awakens him. He glances over at the alarm clock and sees that it's time to get back on the road. He gathers his clothes, guns, and other death producing instruments, and exits his domicile. He steps out into the warm day light. The sun is out in full force. Herrick is back on his mission. He cautiously surveys his surroundings while making his way to his car. He doesn't trust anything. He gets into his car and speeds off. Herrick rolls through the streets with no regard for the rules and regulations of the road. He is a pro at outrunning police and other law enforcement. His car's customized HEMI engine, along with a few other alterations, make it the perfect vigilante mobile. He arrives at his destination. The sign above the storefront reads JOE'S CUP. He parks at a distance and keeps his eyes alert. As he surveys the coffee shop, he takes notice of another important piece to his ultimate plan to bring down Cross. He sees the man he has been looking for, he sees SEAN WEST.

5
THE AWAKENING

For three days, Sean has stayed by Rebecca's side, barely eating or sleeping. He has waited, prayed, and smoked countless cigarettes in the process. Finally, on the fourth day, he notices Rebecca move. He begins calling her name. Her eyelids start to move and eventually, her eyes open. Rebecca stares up at Sean. Her mouth opens, and a faint voice escapes from it.

"Sean?"

"Yes baby I'm here," he responds. His face lights up like a kid on Christmas day. "How are you feeling?" He asks.

"I'm not sure. I'm numb," she responds. Her mind is still foggy. The combination of medication and prolonged slumber has left her groggy.

"So what do you remember?" Sean asks as he gazes at Rebecca with a deep look of warmth, mixed with compassion and concern.

"I don't remember much. All I remember is coming out of the baby boutique. I feel so numb Sean. I don't feel him anymore, I don't feel anything." Rebecca says as tears start trickling down her face. Sean doesn't understand exactly what she is saying, but he knows it isn't good. The moment is interrupted when the doctor walks in. He is a slightly older gentleman with a head of graying thinned hair. He has a kind face with a few noticeable wrinkles.

"Good afternoon Mrs. West. How are you doing today? He smiles at her before turning to Sean. "And I believe you are Mr. West?" He says before extending an open hand towards Sean. "I am Doctor Conivak." He says as the two shake hands. "When I'm done with Rebecca, may I have a word with you outside?" He asks Sean before walking over to Rebecca.

"Sure," Sean responds.

"Great." He says before putting on his stethoscope. Dr. Conivak begins by checking her pulse. After he gets her pulse reading, he checks her heartbeat. He performs a short series of additional tests and notes the results on his a small notepad once they are completed. "Rebecca your vitals look pretty good considering, but I really must let you know that things aren't going to be the same as they were before the accident." He says as he places the notepad inside one of his pockets.

"What do you mean?" Rebecca asks faintly, still trying to regain strength.

"I will discuss everything with you in due time, but first we need to focus on getting your strength up. We will try to get you on solid food in a few days. In the meantime, I need you to get as much rest as possible. The nurse will be in to check on you periodically." He turns to Sean and gestures for him to follow him.

"I will be right back baby." Sean says to Rebecca before following Dr. Conivak out of the room.

"Look Mr. West I don't know how to say this but I'm just going to give it to you straight. We couldn't save the baby...the extent of the injuries were too severe." Sean gasps, "There is also a high possibility of paralysis below the waist, and her ability to conceive and carry to term has been dramatically reduced." Sean is unable to respond. He is in a major state of shock. "Sorry Mr. West, we did all we could." Dr. Conivak says before walking away.

"I know," is all he can say as he tries to digest the news. *"How will Rebecca take this?"* He wonders as he musters up the strength to go back in the room and face her. He goes back in the room, puts on a fake smile, and attempts to act as normal as possible given the circumstances.

"So what did the Doctor say?" Rebecca asks. Sean searches for the right words to say before speaking.

"Well basically...he said to make sure you get plenty of rest and positive support to help speed the recovery process, he also explained the procedures that they will be using to monitor your progress." He hates lying to her, but now is not the time to break the dream shattering news to her. Now is not the time to let her know that fate has given her an extremely unkind hand. Sean knows that he must stay strong for her and allow her to focus on recovering and staying optimistic. He looks into her eyes and still sees the deep warm connection that has helped get them through even the most trying of times. They have faced many storms together. They will face this one together as well but now is not the time for the news. Her spirits must stay high.

"Sean I feel so numb...I know the baby is gone...I can't feel him..." Rebecca has a lost look on her face. "I appreciate you for not wanting to tell me the news, but I'm not as crushed as you or I might have expected. We will try again if we must, it happened once it can happen again right? I'm just happy to be alive. I'm also grateful that have you by my side." Sean reaches closer to hug Rebecca. Tears start to form in both of their eyes as they hold each other. "Ouch, not so tight I'm still sore." Rebecca says with a weak giggle. Her optimism makes him feel even worse about lying.

"Sorry baby," Sean says as he loosens his hold around her. Unbeknownst to Rebecca, he is apologizing for both the overzealous hug and for keeping the damaging news under wraps. "I'm just so happy to see you again. I don't know what I would do without you." He mumbles before giving her a long passionate kiss. "I Love you Rebe."

"I Love you too Sean."

Sean's phone rings. He looks at the screen but doesn't recognize the number. "I wonder who this is, I don't recognize the number?" He says to Rebecca while showing her the number.

"Just answer it and find out baby." She responds. Sean answers the phone.

"Hello?"

"Uh...hey honey...how is my daughter-in-law doing?" He knows the voice on the other end of the line.

"She's doing fine Thelma thanks for your concern." He responds sharply.

"You know I wouldn't mind being called Mom." She says sarcastically.

"You already know how it is, so don't go there! I don't have time deal with this right now so can we please not get into that?"

"I'm just saying Malcolm"

"It's Sean, Thelma. Not Malcolm!"

"I named you that and that's what you will always be to me." Sean walks out of the room. The connection is lost before he can respond.

"Glad she's gone and I pray to God she doesn't come up here." He thinks to himself as he puts his phone back in his pocket. Instead of going right back into the room, he goes to the vending machine to get a cup of coffee. His blood boils hot with rage. He is so close to hating her. He uses every fiber in his being to keep his disdain for her at bay. He reaches the vending machine and runs into his Father. Sean's father is an older black gentleman in his 50's. He has a soft gentle, manly, mostly wrinkle free face. The wrinkles that have taken up residence on it are the result of many worry filled sleepless nights. Seeing his father slightly cools

his rage. He wants to stay mad but the sight of his father triggers a flood of fond loving memories in his mind. The sacrifice that his father made to keep a stable home for Sean and Linda made a lasting impression on Sean. The long days he spent working his fingers to the bone to keep the bills paid and college savings filled, the way that he always made time to help them with their homework. These among many are the many reasons why he will always be a hero to Sean. *"I can't be mad at him I know he meant well by telling her."* Sean thinks to himself as he walks over to his father. The two men shake hands and embrace.

"How are you holding up son?" His father asks while looking into Sean's eyes. He can sense the pain and turmoil festering in his Son. He wishes he could make it better like he's done countless times before when Sean needed him. He wishes he could use his "Dad Powers" to take the burden off Sean. Whenever his children were in a pinch, he would swoop in and save the day. Dad the hero would keep all of life's monsters at bay. He made sure to maintain their household in spite of their mother's absence and all consuming substance abuse. He remembers waking up in the middle of the night to the sounds of her rummaging through the house for any and everything she could sell or trade for drugs. He remembers how she would come in on those nights reeking of cigarettes and cheap cologne. She didn't even try to hide the evidence of her extramarital activities. Sean's father knew she was no longer his. He tried his best not to acknowledge the cold harsh truth. He made sure to keep her demons away from their children.

No matter what it took, he did it. Even if it meant changing the locks, calling the cops, or getting restraining orders against her, he did it for them. Now he feels just as helpless as his son does. His daughter-in-law's world has been disrupted. He was looking forward to being a grandfather. He anxiously anticipated the day he would hear tiny footsteps around his house again, even if only for weekends and occasional visits. Now all of that has been put to screeching halt. Right now, all Mr. West is concerned about is Rebecca and Sean. Poor Rebecca, she just recently suffered the loss of her father and her mother's declining health has only made things that much more unfair; and soon she will have to deal with being disabled and infertile. Life is such the bad card game in the lousy rigged casino. The house always wins.

"Is she up yet?" Mr. West asks before fetching his coffee from the stand near the vending machine.

"Yes." Sean says before blowing into his hot cup of Joe and taking a sip. "Let me take you back to see her. I talked to Linda. She stopped up here earlier. She told me you might be coming by to check on us." Sean says before taking another sip of coffee. He starts to turn to walk.

"Wait," Mr. West says as he places his hand on Sean's shoulder. "Are you alright son?"

"You know what dad to be honest with you, I'm not sure." Sean responds honestly.

"You will be. You have to be, for her...we all have to be for Rebecca." Mr. West says as he looks intently at his son. He can't believe how much his baby boy has changed. It seemed like only yesterday he was helping him take his first steps. Now a full-grown man stands before him, a man going through his own trial by fire. Mr. West smells the faint scent of cigarettes on his son. Sean is back off the wagon, though he can hardly blame him. He would probably be doing the same thing if he were the one going through it.

"I know dad, I'm just glad she made it through."

"Sean you know if you need anything, I'm here and—" Before Mr. West can finish, Sean interrupts.

"Dad I know. You have always been there. Two parents rolled up into one. You have been my father and mother. I'm the man that I am today because of you. You never gave up or gave in, in spite of any circumstances. That same strength is in me. It's in my blood. I'm going to do whatever it takes to make sure me and Rebecca make it through this." A single tear runs down the side of Mr. West's face. Tears begin to bubble up in Sean's eyes as well. Both men understand. Pain is the thing that molds them. Makes them into what they need to be for those that need them the most. "Let me take you back to see Rebecca and sit with us for a while." Sean says as he gestures for his father to follow.

The two men enter the room. Rebecca is wiping the tears from her face. "Is everything alright honey?" Mr. West asks.

"Yeah dad I'm okay." Rebecca responds. He knows she is lying, but given the circumstances that she is dealing with, he understands. Sean rushes to her side.

"Is there anything you need me to get?" He asks.

"When Dad leaves, we need to talk." She responds.

"Okay Rebe,"

"I'm glad to see you're still with us." Mr. West says as he walks over to them. "Like I told Sean, if there is anything you guys need, don't hesitate to ask."

"Alright dad," Rebecca says. She tries to keep a smile on her face to mask the pain and sorrow. Her world is falling to pieces right before her eyes. She feels so helpless and overwhelmed. Lying in the hospital bed brings back memories that she has tried desperately to block out. She remembers waiting and hoping for her dad to make it out of a coma. Images of her bandaged and broken hero lying on the sterile white linen still haunt her psyche. The pain of his death never went away.

"Your Mother might be coming up here to see you guys." Mr. West says.

"I know Dad. I really don't want to talk about her."

"She has changed a lot. She's clean and working and—"

"Dad, please!" Sean interrupts in an agitated manner.

"Okay son." Mr. West says before changing the subject. He begins to talk about old times. Reminiscing on Sean's childhood quickly helps to change the mood in the room. They talk about the first time Sean rode a bike, his first car, the time he broke the neighbor's front window while playing catch. Some of it actually brings out a little laughter amongst the group. Rebecca smiles when Mr. West mentions the first time Sean brought her home for dinner.

"Well I think I need to get going. I gotta do a double shift tomorrow. You know me." Mr. West says as he puts his coat on.

"Now Dad how many times have I told you to take it easy? You don't need the money. I already have one person I love in the hospital. I don't need you there too!" Sean expels in a concerned manner.

"I know son, it's just that if I don't keep myself busy...I'm gonna...I don't know. It helps to keep my mind off things. You know it's just me at the house. You and your sister are living your own lives and—"

"That's because you've based your entire life around us. You stopped living for yourself a long time ago."

"I guess you're right Sean. Before Linda moved back home after she got laid off, I was actually starting to adjust to living for myself."

"Just promise me that once things are back on track, you'll relax and take a well-deserved, long overdue vacation. I mean enjoy your life. Go out and mingle. Find a new Mrs. West!"

"Yeah dad you need to take it easy." Rebecca agrees.

"Well kids, I'll do my best. I can't promise anything right now but I will cut back on working so many hours."

"Okay fair enough pops." Sean says as they both start to get up. Mr. West hugs Sean and Rebecca before leaving. With his Dad gone, Sean sits alone and stares at Rebecca. Rebecca gets straight to the point.

"So what did the doctor say honey?" Sean is conflicted. He was hoping to wait until a later more opportune time to tell her the downright unbearable news.

"Well…it's nothing really Rebe baby." He responds.

"Look Sean rather you tell today or a month from now, I'm still going to have to face it and deal with it. So just tell me." The look on Rebecca's face shows no sign of fear. She is ready to face whatever new cards the dealer known as life has thrown from its obstacle filled deck. Sean doesn't want to lie, but regardless of what Rebecca says, he knows she is in no position to hear any of devastating news.

"He just told me about the meds that they gave you, and how long they expect you to be here. Now I need you to just clear your head and rest up. The sooner you get well and stable, the sooner we can get you outta this place!"

"Are you sure that's all Sean"

"Yes, now let's relax and watch some TV." Sean kisses Rebecca on the forehead and grabs the remote. He turns on the TV and begins flipping through the channels. He finds an edited comedy special. The special has most of the juicy salacious language and humor edited out of it, but they make the best of it. He holds Rebecca's hand until they both drift off to sleep.

The sunrise creeping through the window blinds, awakens Sean. He glances over at Rebecca. She is sleeping peacefully. Her faint snores sound like a rhythmic melody to his ears. He knows her peace is only for a limited time. He knows that once she finds out, she might never recover from the loss. He feels helpless in the position of knowing, it's tearing him apart just thinking about it. Keeping secrets from Rebecca brings back memories of how his father tried to keep his mother's drug addiction a secret. Secrets are like cancer, silent and in most cases deadly. Sean knows he must tell her everything. If she doesn't hear it from him, she will find out from the Doctor. The doctor told Sean because he knew it would only be a matter of time before he would tell Rebecca. He knew it would be best to hear it from a loved one instead of a complete stranger. Sean now realizes this and knows what he must do. He gets himself together and goes out for a quick smoke.

After finally making it the designated area, he takes a Newport 100 out of the box and sparks it up. He inhales the poisonous chemicals and releases the toxic fog of smoke into the air. He continues the process as thoughts run through his mind. With his free hand, he rubs the side of his stubble-filled face. He needs a shave bad. It's been almost a week since a razor has touched his face. He hasn't been able to focus on anything outside of Rebecca's well being. He takes out his phone and scrolls through all of the missed calls and unread text messages. He has been so detached from the world. His mother has been trying to contact him as well, but he refuses to give her the satisfaction of getting him angry. Other than family, he hasn't spoken to anyone. He hasn't contacted his job in days.

At this point, he could care less about the unfulfilling hellhole known as his place of employment. Being in charge of purchasing for a multimillion-dollar company is not what he expected it to be. His father had to slave like a grunt in a dirty dusty factory, just to make his money. Sean is far removed from that environment. He promised himself that he would never settle for blue-collar employment. Now he realizes that every job comes with its own stresses. His job is as draining mentally as his father's is physically. He is in no rush to get back to it. He finishes his cigarette and returns back to the hospital. As he gets closer to Rebecca's room, he can hear a conversation coming from within it. He walks in and see's someone he would rather not. Sean sees his mother next to Rebecca. She looks worn out. The years of drug abuse have taken a tremendous toll on her. Her blond hair is limp and frazzled. Deep bags rest beneath her eyes. She looks healthier now that she is clean off drugs, but the years of self-destruction are still evident. She smiles at Sean as he enters the room.

"Hey honey I was just telling Rebecca about your little brother—" Before his mother can finish her sentence, Sean explodes.

"I thought I told you not to come up here!"

"Malcolm honey can we put our issues aside for the moment c—"

"No we can't put them aside! I have nothing to say to you! I don't want anything to do with you! I don't know that little fucker that is supposed to be my half brother! I'm not Malcolm, she isn't your daughter-in-law, and he's not my brother!" Sean lays into his mother hard. The room grows silent. Sean's eyes are like those of a cornered animal ready to lash out to protect itself. Rebecca turns away. She can't bear to look at Sean in his current state. She knows his pain. She remembers the nights they would stay up talking about his childhood. She understands why he is so hurt. She understands but seeing him like this is the last thing she needs. "You left us, stole from us, hurt us. Kids ridiculed me at school after they saw you get arrested for shoplifting from a fucking Wal-Mart. They called me Son of a klepto, Mutt rag, and Crack baby! That's just some of the names I was called. I was chased home on a regular basis. I got into so many fights I'm surprised that I managed to graduate! My dad was good to you and you fucked around on him, stole from him, and broke his heart! Now you have the nerve to come up here talking about some bastard you had with the dope man you cheated on my father with!

I FUCKING HATE YOU! I HOPE YOU BURN IN HELL!" The words sting Sean's mother like a red-hot poker fresh out of the fire. A nurse hearing the commotion comes into the room.

"Is everything okay?" She asks.

"Everything is fine, she was just leaving!" Sean says as he points to his mother. His mother gets up in a flustered manner, and leaves.

"The Doctor will be in shortly to talk with you." The nurse says before leaving back out. Sean knows that now is the time to tell Rebecca the news.

"Rebe honey, I don't know how to tell you this...there is no easy way. I'm going to tell you the best way possible. When the doctor asked to have a word with me, he told me some things about your condition. He told me that the baby is gone." Sean pushes himself to continue as tears start to form in his eyes. "He also said that there is a huge possibility that you won't be able to conceive and carry to full term." He sees the hurt in her face. He wants to stop but he knows that he must tell her the last bit of it. "And...there is one last thing." He paces himself before releasing it. "You might be partially paralyzed." Sean releases the last bit of crushing news. Each piece of the news is like a blow from a heavyweight prizefighter. Rebecca is left speechless. She feels her world crashing down around her. Shock has left her frozen. Sean rushes over to embrace her. She barely embraces him back. She is in a definite state of shock. Tears burst from Sean's eyes as he holds her. He feels just as crushed as she does. He knows that their world will never be the same.

6
THE HEAT

ROBERT CROSS paces back and forth as he thinks of how he wants to convey exactly how pissed off he is. He has his most trusted associates seated like Knights at the round table. Smoke dances back and forth in the air, escaping from his freshly lit cigar. Unlike most people, he only smokes cigars when he is stressed or angry. When he has a lit cigar, those around him know that it is not a good time to be in his presence. Most of those gathered, have nervous looks on their faces. They know someone is going to get far more than a stern lecture. Cross is a man that few want to piss off or disappoint. As he continues pacing, the room remains silent. No one dares to release the slightest sound into the atmosphere. Once he is sure that he has everyone's undivided attention, Robert breaks the silence.

"Cross King Capital, is seeing a dramatic loss in share prices. Ever since the news of this corporation having ties to the Sin Lords leaked into the media, share prices have dropped by almost thirty-five percent! No one wants to be associated with a corporation that is rumored to have ties to organized crime! This unflattering news will have an effect on all of the companies that we have shares in!" Robert fumes before taking another puff from his cigar. "Jarvis," Robert says as he turns his attention to a specific member seated at the table.

"Yes Mr. Cross," The man responds in a shaky tone.

"I guess it's safe to assume that you're having trouble controlling your street monkeys." Robert states, his gaze becomes slightly aggressive as he focuses on Jarvis.

"With all due respect sir—" Jarvis tries to interject but is quickly cut off.

"I wasn't asking you a question, and I didn't want you to speak. Your fucking monkeys are running wild and harming innocent bystanders! That has a ripple effect and draws heat to us! The media and law enforcement never forget! It's bad enough that we have damn near half a city worth of pigs on payroll. The last thing we need is for more law enforcement to get involved! FBI, CIA, DEA, DOJ, once they get involved, everything is shut down, and the fangs are coming out! I will kill everybody in this room before I go to prison! Jarvis get this situation settled and make this problem disappear! Whichever of your monkeys is responsible, I want their fucking head! I want them to pay for their insolence with blood! I also want the fucking ignorant son of a bitch that goes by the name Blood, dead!" Blood has been a thorn in Robert's side for the longest. With him out of the way, there will be no one left to oppose his rule of the streets. One of the members seated at the table gets up.

"I can't take this anymore! I'm outta of here!" The member, which is a woman, begins to walk towards the door. Robert pulls out pistol and fires. BOOM, the bullet hits the woman before she can reach the door. She falls to the floor with a loud painful thud. Everyone in the room is frozen with fear. The injured woman lies on the hard marble floor with a puddle of blood starting to pool underneath her. No one dares come to her aid. Robert walks over towards his victim with a lit cigar in his hand and a smoking pistol in the other. He reaches the woman. She rolls over and stares at him with wide shock filled eyes.

"H-how could you Robert...what about last night?" The woman questions as life escapes from her.

"What do you mean what about last night? You think just because you gave me some of your fucking cunt that I was going to treat you differently! Well I got news for you baby. No one gets out alive! I put this empire over pussy any day!" BOOM, he pulls the trigger and doesn't even flinch. He turns around and faces the rest of the room. "Somebody get this cleaned up, oh and Jarvis?"

"Y-yes Mr. Cross,"

"Tell Vinnie I want Blood!" He says before walking out.

Some might question why a man so successful in the legitimate business world, would want to still have a strong presence in the seedy underworld. In order to find the logic of such a double life, one must understand Robert's upbringing. Crime is in his blood, his street ties run generations deep. It's a family tradition. From his great grandfather's bootleg liquor operation, to his father's late seventies, early eighties cocaine empire, the Cross name has always been a staple in Garland's underworld. Having such a notorious background makes staying out of the press a job all in itself, especially when you own majority shares of one of the biggest pharmaceutical companies in the country. Robert's company, Cross King Capital, owns shares in several different companies, one of them being the pharmaceutical giant known as Crawford Industries. Robert has his hands in everything, from organized crime to innovative medicine. Dabbling in so many different facets of business has helped Robert keep his sanity and edge. He refuses to give up the streets, no matter how much legitimate success he acquires.

Robert sits alone in his office. A half full glass of expensive Brandy rests before him on his desk. He knows he is crazy. A sane man doesn't just kill one of his lovers in cold blood and act as if it didn't happen. He can't help what he has become. It's too late to change. This life was meant for him. Killing has become second nature to him. *"She had to go. I couldn't let her walk out. I couldn't risk having everything that I've work for go down in flames."* He thinks as a way of rationalizing his actions. Now she has become another ghost in his corrupt, twisted mental index. Her laugh echoes in his head. Her scent haunts his sense of smell. Her sweet, hot sex is no more. Never again will he feel the warmth of her wet sticky lust. He wishes someone else had gotten up instead. He would have gladly killed everyone else in the room if it could have prevented her actions, if it would have barred her demise. Each murder rips another piece of humanity from him. Each time he pulls the trigger, it takes him back to the first time. It takes him back to the cold wet night he graduated from a boy to a monster. He feels tears starting to form. He fights them back with all his might. He can't afford to let what's left of his humanity out in his world. It is a liability with a cost is too great. He grabs the glass of brandy and quickly downs it. The strong sting of the liquor helps him win the fight against the tears. It helps bring the monster back to the forefront. "Fuck that bitch!" he mumbles as slams the glass down on the desk, with a hard clank.

Meanwhile, in a plush decked out penthouse across town, Jay Blood is recuperating. He rests idly in front of a state of the art 3D eighty inch Flat Screen TV. His dark muscular frame is sprawled across a rather expensive black and gray, suede/Italian leather sofa. His dreads hang wild and loose. He keeps finding his attention diverted to the object of his desire. With bruised ribs and his arm in a sling, it will be at least a week or two before he can indulge in one of his most beloved pastimes, shooting pool. He is almost on the verge of lusting after his custom-made pool table. His pool game made a nice hustle when he was kid on the streets of Garland. He made some nice money playing against the drug dealers, pimps, and other degenerates of Garland's underworld.

His mind shifts to another need, companionship. He contemplates calling over one of his female friends for a quick fix, but he's not really in the mood. He is still in shock. He can't believe that he is the only member of his squad left. He knows his big brother Blood is not pleased to say the least, especially considering the fact that he almost lost his only brother due to something so stupid and hotheaded. He understands that once he makes a full recovery, Blood will want him to stay out of the streets for a while, at least until things cool down and the proper channels are appeased. He reflects on his near death experience as he flips through random cable channels. It has been so long since he has had downtime that it is really getting to him. He doesn't dare defy Blood. His brother has been his protector ever since they lost both of their parents at the hands of a young Robert Cross.

The pain of their deaths, still live with them. Jay's mind drifts back to that dark wet night in April nearly two decades ago. He remembers his mother tucking him in and kissing his forehead for the last time. He can still hear the gunshots and her screams. He remembers escaping out of his bedroom window with his older brother. It was only by the grace of God that they avoided death that night. Shortly after, their aunt and uncle took them in. Their aunt and uncle lived in a stable middleclass neighborhood and were God-fearing hardworking citizens. In spite of their deliverance from a violent urban environment, the brothers still found themselves living the same crime influenced lifestyle that their father lived before them.

Jay sits stuck in time, drowning his sorrows in his favorite drink of choice, Red Bull and Vodka, no ice, and mostly Vodka, with only a squirt of bull. He likes to feel the sting as it courses down his throat. In mid gulp, he hears something outside of his apartment. He pauses, and softly places his drink down on its coaster. He slowly turns down the volume on the TV. As he is doing so, he hears more noise from outside of his door. He slowly reaches for a pistol nestled in between the couch cushion and armrest. He cautiously makes his way to his apartment's entrance. He reaches the door, and peeks through the peephole. He does not see anything. Wanting to get a better view, he readies his firearm, and carefully starts to open the door. While opening the door, someone rushing towards catches him off guard. Jay instinctively aims his gun and wraps his finger around the trigger. He stops himself from squeezing the trigger, once he realizes who it is. It is Tia his on again off again love interest. Her soft medium brown skin glows with sex appeal

"Whoa, you almost got your head blown off girl. What the fuck are you doing here?" He says, as he looks at her. Her warm seductive smile quickly tames his aggressive demeanor.

"Baby I just wanted to surprise you," she responds, as she gets closer to him

"You know I don't like surprises," he retorts.

"Well you're gonna love this one," she says before gesturing to someone down the hall. Jay Blood doesn't know what to expect.

Seconds later, a slightly curvaceous blond with ice blue eyes, comes to the door. "Jay this Amber, and Amber, this is Jay."

"Hey how you doing," Amber says in a sexy sultry voice.

"Well that all depends on what the both of you are here for." Jay Blood responds.

"How about you let us in and find out?" Tia says flirtatiously. Jay Blood obliges her requests and lets both women inside.

7
SOME HOPE LEFT

Rebecca is still trying to come to terms with the devastating news. She is better but not fully recovered. She still has a ways to go. Her road to rehabilitation has just begun. She is trying her best to stay strong in spite of the circumstances. She needs to be strong. She keeps a fake smile and false optimism projected to everyone around her, but on the inside, a war rages. She can feel anger and hopelessness, starting to fester and take root in her soul. Her spirit is crushed, but she hides it all from Sean. She has to be strong for him. At this point, it is not even about her anymore. She knows that it is weighing heavily upon him. Today is the first day of the rest of their lives. Today is the day Rebecca returns home. Sean has already hired someone to assist her while he is at work. Everything around them is ready. The only problem is that they aren't. Rebecca does not feel comfortable with the ideal of needing assistance with ordinary things that she had previously taken for granted. Preparing a meal, taking a bath, going to the bathroom, the change is pride shattering. For the rest of her life, she will most likely need assistance, and will have to live with the loss of what could have been. She will forever mourn the precious life that was extinguished before its time.

All of these thoughts go through Rebecca's mind as she sits in the waiting area anxious to leave the sterilized smells, and starched white linens behind. She can see the front parking area through the glass double doors. She sees Sean pull up. Sean comes in and wheels her out to the curb. He then lifts her from out of the wheel chair and into the passenger side. He buckles her in and the two of them head home.

"I know you're glad to finally be outta there." Sean says as an attempt to strike up conversation.

"Yeah that hospital food left much to be desired!" Rebecca replies. "I've been hankering for some McDonalds"

"You mean McNasty's?" Sean jokes as turns onto a main intersection.

"Very funny, I'm serious! Can you stop by one? The closest one is like two minutes up the street." Rebecca replies. Sean thinks about it. Even though he is opposed to eating the stuff, he is happy to have her out of the hospital so he will oblige her request.

"I'm just playing with you babe, of course I'll take you there. I know exactly what you want too!"

"Oh really, then what do I want psychic friend?" Rebecca asks sarcastically.

"You want a ten piece Mcnugget meal with fresh fries, no salt, and a Root beer."

"No actually, I only want a six piece!" She jokes as they both begin to laugh. Moments like these give Sean hope.

"I love you Rebe." Sean says as he places his hand on her thigh. Remembering her new condition, he quickly pulls it away.

"It's okay baby." Rebecca says as she grabs his hand and places it back on her leg. She forces a smile on her face to keep him at ease, but deep down she feels like shit. She imagines herself receiving assistance for her condition, and the notion doesn't sit well with her. She feels a deep hatred growing from within.

"If the city had done a better job at keeping the streets safe, I wouldn't have gotten injured." She thinks as she stares out of the window. "I think we should sue the city." She says in a serious tone.

"Huh," Sean responds.

"I think we should sue them for allowing those criminals to run the streets and harm innocent lives, our lives!" Rebecca says as she turns to look at Sean.

"Okay I understand how you feel honey. First, we have to find a lawyer that will take on such a case. Sean replies. "We can call around today and see." He says as they pull up to the McDonalds.

"Hello welcome to McDonalds. Would you like to try our new Chicken select?" The drive thru attendant says through the intercom as Sean pulls up.

"Uh, no thank you. Let me get a six piece Mcnugget meal and I want the fries with no salt and the nuggets fresh."Sean says

"What type of drink would you like with your meal sir?" The attendant asks.

"Root Beer with very little ice," he responds

"Okay will that complete your order?" The attendant asks.

"Yes that's all." Sean replies. The attendant gives him his total and he pulls around to pay. After paying, they pull to the second window and the drive thru attendant tells them that it's a wait on the Mcnuggets and fresh fries. They pull into the designated area and wait. Sean is itching to smoke but knowing how much Rebecca is against it, he curbs his urge and decides to wait until they make it home before satisfying it. They sit in awkward silence waiting for the food. Sean thinks about the possibility of them actually suing the city while Rebecca has a flashback of the accident. Remembering the point of impact makes her jump. "Are you okay?" Sean asks

"Do I look okay?" Rebecca snaps as an involuntary reflex. "I'm sorry Sean it's just—"

"No need to explain. I understand." He responds. "We're gonna get through this baby." Sean says as he smiles at his better half.

One of the restaurant staff finally brings out Rebecca's meal. She checks it to make sure it is right, and they leave. While driving past a store on the way home, Sean notices an ad for legal assistance. *"Lawsuits, Medical Malpractice, Wrongful Death, we deal with it all call: 216-555-6868 Phillips & Associates"*

He slows down and tells Rebecca to write down the number. She calls immediately.

"Hello the law offices of Phillips & Associates, Traci speaking how may I help you?"

"Hi my name is Rebecca West and I'm interested in legal services."

"Pardon my asking, but are you the lady that was struck by an out of control vehicle?"

"Yes how did you know?"

"The news, they have been giving updates on your story for the past three weeks."

"Oh okay."

"I can schedule you for a free consultation. We have a few openings available."

"Okay well what is the soonest that you have available?"

"Well Mrs. West we actually have an opening for tomorrow at eleven fifteen. Does that work for you?"

"Um yes that will work." The woman types Rebecca's name into the scheduling program.

"Okay Mrs. West, I have you down for eleven fifteen. Now all I ask is that you arrive at least fifteen minutes early to fill out paperwork, and bring two forms of ID."

"Alright,"

"Okay Mrs. West, we will see you tomorrow have a good day."

"You do the same." Rebecca ends the call.

"So we're going to see the attorney tomorrow?" Sean asks as

he turns onto their street.

"Yup," Rebecca responds as she saves the number and appointment in her phone. They finally reach their home. Sean pulls into the driveway. He exits the car and pops the truck to remove the wheelchair and get it ready for Rebecca. He wheels it around to the passenger side, opens the door, and nervously attempts to get her out.

"It's okay Sean I'm not a fragile piece of glass." Rebecca jokes as a way to help Sean relax. He successfully manages to get her into the wheelchair. They make their way into the house.

"It's a good thing this place already has a ramp." Sean says as he closes the door. Sean heads straight upstairs. Rebecca wheels herself into the front room. It is hard for her to believe that she has been in the hospital for nearly three weeks. She feels so strange being back home. It all seems foreign. It seems like only yesterday, she was in the kitchen making breakfast. Everything almost looks exactly as she left it. The mug that she drank orange juice out of before leaving on that tragic day still rests on the coffee table. The sight of it triggers flashbacks in her mind. Out of anger, she grabs the mug and flings it across the room. It hits the wall and shatters on impact.

Sean is trying to hold it together as he gathers up all of the baby stuff. He fights back his tears as he shoves item after item into a garbage bag. The sound of something shattering brings out his alertness. His mind shifts to Rebecca. "Is everything okay?" He yells.

"Yes honey, I just dropped a mug." Rebecca yells back as she looks at the pieces. She knows it's going to be hell adjusting to this new life. Based on the reaction triggered by the sight of the mug, she cannot even bring herself to imagine going into the baby's room. Sean enters the room.

"Hey babe, are you sure everything is okay?" He asks as the broken mug catches his attention.

"Yes honey. Well, not exactly. I'm going to need you to get rid of all of the stuff in the room." She cannot even will herself to utter the word baby. It does not matter. Sean already knows which room she is referring.

"I've already started." He responds, "Try to relax. If you need anything, just call me. I'm going to get back to it." He says before walking over and placing a kiss on Rebecca's forehead. Sean turns to walk away. Rebecca grabs his hand.

"Baby wait," she says as their eyes connect. "I, I love you. And I just want to say thank you for staying by my side and being so supportive."

"Well the vows said for better or for worse, in sickness and in health so I'm here for the long haul. Oh and I love you too Rebe." He says before smiling at her and leaving the room. His cigarettes are calling him. He steps outside and immediately lights up. The smoke helps to comfort his nerves. He takes deep puffs. He feels his hand shaking as he raises and lowers the lit cigarette. He still is angry over what happened. "*Where is the justice?*" He ponders as he takes the last drag off the cigarette. He feels hopeless and overwhelmed. He has a good job but until Rebecca's disability kicks in, the expenses are going to have a definite impact on their lifestyle. "Stupid fucking thugs," He fumes as he exhales the last of the smoke. He has had enough of everything. He feels so tired and burned out, and desperately wants to give in to the stresses of life, but he forces himself to stay strong instead. He has to stay strong for Rebecca's sake. She needs him more than ever. He is still struggling to adjust to the dramatic change. He shakes off his moment of weakness and goes back inside to finish gathering the rest of the baby stuff.

He manages to gather all of the baby's belongings. All that remains is the baby blue paint and the cutesy wallpaper border. After clearing out the room, he is too tired to undertake that task. He just wants to lie down in his nice warm bed and get some rest. He knows that his desire for rest might be difficult to fulfill considering Rebecca's condition, so instead of getting rest, he goes to the refrigerator and grabs out an energy drink. The aid staff will arrive tomorrow to take some of the load off his shoulders, but for now, he has to finish up with the room and keep an eye on Rebecca. He finishes his drink and goes into the basement. He grabs the first can of paint that he finds. The paint is some off white color. He picks up the rest of the supplies, and heads back upstairs. He is aching for another cigarette. He doesn't even bother going outside to smoke. The window is already open so he lights up and handles his fix. The chemicals in the cigarette give him a head rush. It calms him and helps him sort out his thoughts. He finishes his cigarette and throws himself into his work.

The sun starts to set as Sean applies the last strokes of paint. He finishes, cleans up the room, and makes his way back down to check on Rebecca and clean himself up.

"Hey honey is everything alright?" He asks as he enters the room. As he gets closer to her, he realizes that she is asleep. He sits next to Rebecca and drifts off to sleep.

8
WHERE'S THE JUSTICE?

Sean and Rebecca pull up to the Office of Phillips and Associates. He is glad that they aren't located downtown. The parking situation in Downtown Garland is horrible. The lots charge astronomical fees for parking and the meter maids are always on the prowl. Sean helps Rebecca out of the car and wheels her to the door. A young woman in the waiting area sees them coming up to the door and assists them in. The waiting area decorated nicely. An arrangement of plagues, various awards, and certifications adorn its walls. A large fish tank rests in an area next to the receptionist's desk. Guest chairs fill in the majority of the space. Sean picks an end seat and rolls Rebecca next to it. He then goes up to the receptionist. "Hi I'm Sean West. My wife and I have a scheduled appointment to see Attorney Cooper." Sean says

"Hello Mr. West." She says while typing and focusing her attention on her computer screen. "I see your appointment sir. I have a few papers that I need you and your wife to fill out." She hands him the paperwork and a clipboard with a pen attached to it. "Now once you're done, bring it back up and Attorney Cooper will see you shortly."

"Thank you." Sean says as he takes the papers and seats himself next to Rebecca. They complete the paperwork, and Sean returns it back to the receptionist. "Hey Rebe, I'm about to go have a quick smoke." Sean says as gets up. Rebecca wants to protest but she stops herself. She understands that her current situation is affecting him as well. It is a lot of stress on the both of them.

"Okay," is all that she mutters. "I will call or text you if they call us before you get back." She adds.

"Alright," Sean responds as he starts walking toward the exit. Sean steps outside and pulls a slightly crumpled pack of Newports from out of his pocket. He lifts cigarette box flap and what he sees surprises him. "Damn I'm down to my last two?" He exclaims with shock in his tone. He failed to realize how much he has been smoking until now. He remembers when he was up to a pack a day. *"How can I go almost a year without smoking, and then relapse?"* He thinks as he removes one of the cigarettes. He lights his vice and satisfies his craving. Once he is done, he flicks away the butt and returns to the law office.

"Mrs. West?" A woman in a dark tan business suit calls out as Sean enters the building. Other than a few slight wrinkles, her skin is flawless. She has auburn colored shoulder length hair with sprinkles of gray. She smiles as she looks over the people in the waitin area.

"Yes" Rebecca responds. The lady walks over to her.

"Hello I'm attorney Cooper. I will be conducting your consultation today." She says as she extends her hand.

"Hello Mrs. Cooper." Rebecca responds as the two shake hands. Sean walks over to Rebecca and Attorney Cooper. "This is my husband Sean." Rebecca acknowledges Sean. Sean and Attorney Cooper shake hands as well.

"If you folks will be so kind as to follow me back to my office, we can begin." Attorney Cooper leads them back through a wide hallway adorned with various art pieces and portraits. They reach Cooper's office. Cooper's office has the trappings of a typical attorney's office. Library Cabinetries are stationed on two of the walls. They are filled with numerous volumes and versions of legal tomes. Framed newspaper clippings from past victories, along with certifications and licenses, hang conspicuously for potential clients to see. A well-organized desk rests in the center of the semi spacious room. A comfortable leather office chair sits behind it. Two cozy guest chairs in the front of it. Cooper shows them in and moves one of the guest chairs to accommodate Rebecca. Attorney Cooper tries not to stare at Rebecca but she can't it. She feels sympathy for the crippled beauty. After helping to situate Rebecca and Sean, Attorney Cooper seats herself in her comfortable throne. She takes a moment to gloss over the filled out paperwork before speaking.

"So, Mr. and Mrs. West, it says here that the reason for your visit is that you want to sue the city for negligence and personal injury."

"Yes, that's correct." Sean responds.

"Well according to the new guidelines that were put into place last year, crime victims who suffer physical and/or emotional injury may be eligible for financial assistance from the state's **Victim Compensation Program.** This includes any losses or fees accrued due to the incident, not covered by insurance or other means. Family members or members of the victim's household may also be eligible for assistance as *derivative victims.* Losses covered by this program include medical and dental expenses, mental health counseling, funeral and burial costs, loss of financial support, wages or income, and job retraining expenses (if employed). Limited funds for relocation and/or home security measures may also be available. The loss of personal property or cash is not covered. Now in order for you to be eligible, you must have reported the crime to the presiding law enforcement agency, the victim must cooperate in the investigation, and prosecution of anyone suspected of committing the crime. The victim must also cooperate with the State's Board of Control staff and/or local Victim-Witness Assistance Center personnel in the claim verification process. Now basically, the state will pay you a minimum assistance amount until your case against the city is decided. Here's the tricky part, the city will fight you tooth and nail for every red cent. They will do everything in their power to make sure you receive as little of a settlement as possible! On the other hand, due to the nature of your case, it will definitely get major attention. The attention will definitely work in your favor. Now before you consider proceeding with the process, I must warn you, be prepared for a lengthy battle. Our firm will represent you with no upfront fee required. We will only receive our fee in the event of a victory, so if we don't win, we don't eat. We have excellent expertise in this area. Okay I think I've said a mouthful, so now I want to hear from you. Do you have any questions or any concerns?" Sean's mind stirs as he tries to sort through the information. Rebecca speaks.

"How long will it take to get any compensation from the state?"

"If you were to file today, you would probably get a preliminary date set for anywhere from one to three months from now. Now in conjunction with filing with the courts, we would also send all of your paperwork to the state. Keep in mind that even though we would send it immediately, the benefits will take anywhere from three to four weeks to process. The first ones that you would receive are minimum medical, voucher for security purposes, and a fraction of wage losses. Now once the case has been fully assessed you will get most of what I previously stated. Now if and when you win your case against the city, you will receive a settlement and full payment of medical debts."

"Okay and what are we supposed to do until then?" Rebecca asks.

"Well if you guys are really in a bind, the county may be able to offer you temporary assistance until then. I mean I don't know all of the details of your situation, but I would definitely look into that."

"Alright well first things first, I would like to get things going right away. So let's get started."

"Okay I need to you both to fill out some additional paperwork and then it's a go." The couple nod in agreement and Attorney Cooper goes into one of the drawers of her desk and pulls out the necessary paperwork.

9

BLOOD IS THICKER THAN MONEY

"I'm ready to get back out there bruh," Jay Blood says in between exhaling puffs of marijuana off his freshly lit blunt. His wounds have healed and his anger is a burning fire. He's ready to get back in the game.

"Look Jay, I know you're probably bored out of your mind laying low, but you're all that I got left. Things are too hot right now. The law is really putting heat on us in the streets and I got word that Robert Cross has declared it blood season. Three of our best movers have been gunned down in the last week alone, plus with the drought on "King", the Kilos are higher than a kite on a windy day!" The older Blood says, desperately trying to convince his younger brother Jay Blood into continuing to lay low.

"Big bro I know you just being concerned for me, but our family gotta stay eating, we need to keep our hold on the streets. I need to put my all into it just as much as you, this thing we built is blood in, and no way out but up!" Jay Blood passionately states as he continues to smoke.

"Alright I feel you my nig, just give it another week, hopefully by then this drought will be over and we can go back to business as usual. You know how we do it."

"Okay I'll give it another week, but soon as this week is up, I'm back to punching the clock."

"Alright, now get back to taking five. Call up some freaks and have em' come through and set it out one time."

"You read my mind!" Jay Blood says as he chuckles, "I'm bout to make that move so Imma hit back in a few."

"Cool."

Jay Blood ends the call and quickly scrolls through his list of contacts. He contemplates his choices before picking one. "Hell yeah," he says as he selects Tia. The phone begins to ring. Jay Blood begins to fantasize while he waits for the other end to pick up.

"Hello," a sweet voice interrupts the ringing, and brings Jay Blood's mind back into the real world.

"Hey honey, I need some company what you doing?"

"Nothing just sitting here bored outta my mind,"

"Me too, so how about you and your girl come over here and we find something to do together," Jay Blood says as a smile begins to form on his face. He remembers the last time Tia paid him a visit. He remembers the way her sweet sex game kept him at attention for three rounds. He also remembers her sexy friend Amber joining in. It was one of the best nights of his life.

"Well do you want me to see what Amber's doing, or do you want something new?"

"It don't matter who comes with you just as long as you cum," Jay Blood says slyly infusing a sexual innuendo.

"You know Imma do that baby. The way you be doing it, you be working it like a nigga that's been locked down for ten!"

"Ha, ha you a fool for that one,"

"I'm just saying baby, I don't know if I want anybody else to get another sample of that good bar. I feel like being selfish." Tia says with a slight giggle. She feels herself getting aroused at the thought of Jay Blood being inside of her. She bites her lip as thoughts of the big strong chocolate stallion dance in her head.

"Awww baby you know I got enough to share, plus I don't ever do anybody else as good as do you!" Jay Blood states before taking a hit off his blunt, which has now become a roach. He puts the roach in an ashtray, grabs his signature Vodka mixed drink, and takes a sip.

"I know daddy I know. Imma hit Amber and see what she doing, so call me back in like ten okay?" Tia says.

"Alright," Jay Blood responds before hanging up. Having set up his company, his mood has turned from bored to jovial. He finishes his drink and goes over to his pool table.

Meanwhile on the other side of town, Amber is deeply engaged in a hot sweaty moment with Vinnie, one of Jay Blood's rivals, one of the Sin Lords.

"Oh yeah right there right there,'" Amber exasperates as she wildly throttles Vinnie's slender Italian tan frame. His black hair is drenched in sex-induced sweat. His eyes are filled with an intense lust as he watches Amber grind on top of him. His boyish looks are reminiscent of the innocent boy next-door archetype. Despite his less than intimidating physical stature, Vinnie is as cutthroat as they come.

"Yeah ride this fucking Italian stallion," he shouts as he keeps a slightly firm grip on Amber's backside. The buxom blond grinds and groans passionately as her fierce blue eyes capture the full sexual energy of the moment. She looks exactly as one would expect a stripper to look, cheap, saucy, wicked, and tantalizingly irresistible.

"I'm almost there," she professes before exploding in a rush of satisfaction.

"Oh fuck," Vinnie says as he follows suit. Amber's cell phone begins to ring as she dismounts. She rolls over and grabs it from off the nightstand.

"Hello," she says, partially out of breath.

"Hey girl it's Tia, you feel like having some fun and making a little extra change?"

"Hold on give me a moment," Amber says as she regains her composure. The line goes silent. Tia assesses the condition of her fingernails as she waits.

"I definitely need to get my nails redone." She thinks as she continues looking them over. With Tia on hold, Amber quickly

171

scurries to the bathroom.

"Hey you still there," Amber asks as she closes the bathroom door behind her.

"Yeah bitch I'm still here, if it was an emergency I would be dead by now!" Tia jokes.

"Well you called at the wrong time. I told you I was having company today." Amber says while plopping down on the toilet seat.

"Oh yeah… well anyway, I need you to come with me over to Jay Blood's place."

"Uh well see about that, I don't know if I would be able to do that…"

"What's wrong?" Tia quizzes as she shuffles through her walk-in closet.

"Nothing just—" Amber pauses as she hears the sound of someone on the other side of the door. "Hey let me call you right back." She says before quickly ending the call. Amber flushes the toilet, and opens the door. She comes face to face with Vinnie. Amber steps back, and fakes as if he caught off guard. "Oh, hey honey. You just scared the mess out of me!" She proclaims while placing her hand on her chest.

"Why would you be scared if you know that I'm here? I mean unless you're doing something that you have no business doing. Who were you talking to?"

"I… what makes you think that I was talking to someone?"

"Well for one, I heard your voice, and you answered you

phone before you went into the bathroom remember?"

"Oh yeah," she looks down as she tries to think of a quick lie. "It was nothing, one of my friends just called to talk my ear off." Vinnie looks at her with an intense stare.

"Bitch, don't lie to me! If I find out your fucking with someone else," he grabs her by the throat, "I know about the shit that you and your friends get into. As a matter of fact, I bet I know exactly which hoe it was too!" He tightens his grip on her throat. Amber struggles unsuccessfully to get out of his grip.

"Baby what are you doing, I love you. I would never do anything to hurt you." She manages to eke out in between struggling to breathe.

"Oh really, you do huh?" He releases her, "Well I need you to prove just how much you love me."

10
VENGEANCE

Jay Blood has just gotten out of the shower when his phone begins to ring. He does a rush job at drying off before grabbing it. He puts it on speaker. "Hello," He says as he resumes drying himself.

"Hey baby we're here, buzz us in." Tia says.

"Alright," Jay says before walking over to his the intercom device. He presses the button and goes back to getting ready.

Tia and Amber enter the building. "So are you ready to party girl," Tia questions as they walk towards the elevator.

"Yeah girl you know me." Amber responds in a not so genuine manner. The confrontation earlier with Vinnie is eating at her. She loves him and she is going to prove it today. She feels nervous as she steps inside of the elevator.

"Is everything alright?" Tia asks while pressing the button for the top floor.

"Yeah, I'm just a little tired I guess. My on again off again came by and you know…"

"Damn hoe you don't let your pussy rest for shit do you?" Tia jokes as she smiles at one of her closest friends. She has known Amber since she first arrived in Garland. She was a runaway from a broken home looking for some sense of love, and Amber was a novice exotic dancer looking for a way out. They met after Tia was caught shoplifting. Amber knew the storeowner and offered to pay for the stolen goods. She then convinced Tia to begin dancing, and the two have been tight ever since. Amber knows that what she is about to do might ruin their friendship, but it will save their lives! As the elevator makes its way up to their destination, the events that happened earlier replay in Amber's head…

"Well you called at the wrong time. I told you I was having company today." Amber says while plopping down on the toilet seat.

"Oh yeah… well anyway, I need you to come with me over to Jay Blood's place."

"Uh well see about that, I don't know if I would be able to do that…"

"What's wrong?" Tia quizzes as she shuffles through her walk-in closet.

"Nothing just—" Amber pauses as she hears the sound of someone on the other side of the door. "Hey let me call you right back." She says before quickly ending the call. Amber flushes the toilet, and opens the door. She comes face to face with Vinnie. Amber steps back, and fakes as if he caught off guard. "Oh, hey

honey. You just scared the mess out of me!" She proclaims while placing her hand on her chest.

"Why would you be scared if you know that I'm here? I mean unless you're doing something that you have no business doing. Who were you talking to?"

"I... what makes you think that I was talking to someone?"

"Well for one, I heard your voice, and you answered you phone before you went into the bathroom remember?"

"Oh yeah," she looks down as she tries to think of a quick lie. "It was nothing, one of my friends just called to talk my ear off." Vinnie looks at her with an intense stare.

"Bitch, don't lie to me! If I find out your fucking with someone else," he grabs her by the throat, "I know about the shit that you and your friends get into. As a matter of fact, I bet I know exactly which hoe it was too!" He tightens his grip on her throat. Amber struggles unsuccessfully to get out of his grip.

"Baby what are you doing, I love you. I would never do anything to hurt you." She manages to eke out in between struggling to breathe.

"Oh really, you do huh?" He releases her, "Well I need you to prove just how much you love me."

"I love you enough to do anything for you baby." Amber says nervously.

"Okay well I know about what you and friend Tia did with that piece of shit Blood—"

"How did—"

"Don't worry about how I found out. I just need you to prove how much you love me, so if you really love me, you will set it up so that I can take that bastard out! He killed some of my best men!"

"Okay… just don't hurt Tia."

"Don't worry baby, she's taken care of."

The ding of the elevator bell brings Amber back to the present. "Are you sure you're gonna be up for this, I mean you don't have to fuck but I at least need you to be able to put on a show for him. You know Jay got money on it." Tia says as she studies Amber. She can tell something about her friend is off.

"Give me a drink and a few hits off a blunt and I'll be ready to dance my ass off." Amber responds as she forces a smile. The women step out of the elevator and into a long hallway. The discussion she had with Vinnie begins replaying in her head.

"I'm going to follow you to Tia's place. Once you pick her up, I'm going to be tailing you from a few cars behind. When you get to Blood's apartment, make sure you go up to his floor with Tia, then pretend like you left something in the car and come down and let me in. You got it?"

"Yeah… I got it, but what if she suspects that I had something to do with it?"

"Don't worry about it, I got it covered. Just make sure you do your part okay?"

"Okay,"

Amber's mind comes back to the present. "You know what, I

think I left something in the car," She says in full cooperation of the plan.

"What did you leave?"

"It's a surprise, I brought a little something extra for the show we're about to put on for Jay, I'll be right back."

"Do you want me to go back down with you and hold the door or give you a hand?" Tia asks. She is puzzled as to what Amber has planned on doing. *"She didn't mention it earlier,"* she thinks as she waits for a response.

"No, you go and get Jay ready I got it covered."Amber responds before rushing back to the elevator. She manages to catch it just in time.

Once in the elevator, an intense nervousness overtakes her. She has second thoughts about going through with it. She wishes that she'd never answered Tia's call earlier. She knows that Vinnie is a stone cold killer and that Tia is really feeling Jay. She knows that getting him setup will definitely put a wedge in their relationship. The elevator reaches the first floor and panic sets in full time. Amber feels like going out of another exit and sneaking to her car but she knows that it would result in dire consequences. Vinnie is a man that few have crossed and lived to tell about it. She takes a deep breath and clears her mind before stepping off the elevator. She involuntarily shakes as she makes her way to the door. She sees Vinnie's car through the glass door, as she gets closer to the entrance. Vinnie sees her and gets his pistol ready. He tucks it inside his coat and makes his way to the door. Amanda opens the door and Vinnie steps in.

"Hey baby," he says as he steps inside. He gives her a quick kiss and proceeds to the elevator. Amber stuck in a state of shock, just stands by the door, and looks off in the distance. "C'mon babes," He commands. Amber snaps out of her trance, and reluctantly follows.

"Do I really have to follow you? I can tell you exactly which suite he's in... I mean you're already inside so—,"

"I said come on!" Vinnie says in a cold forceful manner. The look in his eyes sends a chill through her. She can't believe that he is the same man that she was just giving her all to hours earlier. The elevator reaches the floor and Vinnie gets in, followed by Amber. "Which floor is it?"

"I got it," Amber says as she reaches over and presses one of the buttons. As the elevator closes, she feels a lump start to form in her throat. She looks down at her hands and notices that they are slightly shaking. She can't bring herself to look at Vinnie. She just looks down at the floor as the elevator continues its trek up. Amber feels displaced as flashbacks of Jay Blood haunt her thoughts. She remembers every detail of their wild time together with Tia. She can practically smell Jay's scent. *"My mind is really fucking with me!"* She thinks as the images continue to invade her mind. She feels guilty for having them while in the presence of Vinnie. She shutters at the thought of how he would react if he knew what she was thinking. The elevator finally reaches its final destination.

"Get off." Vinnie instructs as he removes his weapon. Amber

hesitantly steps into the hallway. "You take lead down the hall and I will follow, you got it?"

"Please don't hurt her." Amber says, finally mustering up the courage to look at Vinnie.

"I'm only here to take care of one person, she's not my target," Is his cold emotionless response.

Relieved by his response, Amber begins to walk. The walk down the hall seems like the longest walk ever for Amber. She feels like a death row inmate on their way to execution, the only difference is, it is someone else's day to die. After an emotionally agonizing walk, Amber reaches Jay Blood's suite. Vinnie trails behind slowly. He stays far enough to avoid detection. Amber knocks softly on the door. Vinnie quickly makes his way to the intercept. A few seconds later, Tia opens the door.

"H—," before Tia can finish greeting her friend, she comes face to face with a silencer pistol.

"Don't make a sound or your DEAD!" Vinnie whispers in a deathly tone.

"Hey Tia what's the hold up? Is that Amber?" Jay Blood yells from inside the apartment.

"Amber," Vinnie whispers as he gestures her to speak up.

"Yeah I'm here sexy," Amber announces as she steps into the apartment with Vinnie.

"Say one word and I'll blow you're fucking head off!" Vinnie warns Tia as they walk further into the apartment. "Turn around and walk your pretty ass towards him!" He says as he grabs her roughly around her neck. Vinnie is in full rage. The moment of vengeance is so close that he can practically taste it! They continue to walk towards the back bedroom. Jay Blood anxiously waits for the show to begin. He remembers how much fun he had the last time Tia and Amber paid him a visit. He delights as his brain replays all of the scenes like clips from a movie. Tia, a few feet away from the master bedroom, frantically thinks of a way to alert Jay Blood without getting her head blown off in the process. She doesn't want Jay Blood to die but she values her own life more. She knows that anything she attempts will lead to certain death.

"Damn, why does this type of thing have to happen to me?" She thinks as she nears the room. Her heart beats hard and fast as she reaches out to open the door. Before she gets a chance to touch the door, it swings open. Time seems to slow down as Jay Blood comes into view. Amber watches in shock as everything unfolds before her like a scene out of a movie. Vinnie yanks Tia aside. Jay Blood's eyes get wide as saucers as Vinnie comes into view. He turns to retreat into the room as Vinnie's finger squeezes the pistol's trigger. The pistol quietly releases a bullet. In the blink of an eye, it tears into Jay Blood's shoulder.

"Aah," He says as he sloppily darts further into the room. Tia begins to scream as Vinnie forces her into the room with him. Amber stands frozen outside of the room and doesn't witness the finale. The muted sounds of Vinnie's pistol firing shots and Tia's screams resonate from inside the room. Then in an instant, everything goes deathly silent. Seconds later, Vinnie emerges from the room. He has sprinkles of blood on his face and clothes. He stops and looks at Amber. Amber snaps out of her catatonic state, as their eyes lock.

"Tia," is all she can manage to murmur.

"If you say anything, you're dead!" He says before turning and running away.

Mr. Rosette

PROLOGUE

"Go away!" I scream at the top of my lungs, all the while hoping that Heaven, Hell, and everything in between will hear. I know what these things in my house want. They want me! It's not all in my head. It can't be all in my head, they're here right now. My dreams are coming true, unfortunately not in a pleasant way. I can see my breath in front of me as it escapes my warm ninety-eight degree body. I feel the sting of the cold numbing air. The temperature in the room has dropped significantly. Death or something like it is present. Max stands near me paralyzed with alertness; his fur is standing on end, his growl guttural. I feel an icky crawling sensation invade the surface of my skin as goose bumps form on it. I'm flooded with intense fear as I stare deep into something that is there but not there. A shadowy semitransparent creature with red piercing eyes stands in front of me. Its eyes are like small intense fires burning their way into my core. I feel helpless and alone. I know that there is no way to escape; this is it.

I wish Aiden were here. I wish I had his protective courage to rescue me in my darkest hour.

"It is your time, you must transcend. You must become what we need you to be. Spill the blood of the unworthy one and fulfill the divination. He is near. Sacrifice him to your cause." The menacing figure says in unison with the others surrounding me. Who or what they are referring to is unclear. I feel their strong cold hands grab my wrists. I attempt to break free, but my efforts are futile. The more I struggle, the stronger they become.

"No, get off of me!" I yell while struggling for freedom. Suddenly, the creature that I'm directly facing removes its hood and reveals its identity. It is... me! We appear to be the same person, which is utterly impossible. *"How can there be two?"* I ponder as my heartbeat intensifies. My other self, has a sinister look of glee. It is as if she is feeding off my fear.

I never really did take much stock in ghosts, demons, angels, or the paranormal world at large. I figured that only people craving attention or afflicted with mental illness believed in those types of things. Now I don't know what to believe. I really thought that ghost-hunting shows were just a bunch of Hollywood hyped entertainment. Orbs, EVPs, doors opening, mysterious footsteps, haunting reoccurring dreams; these things didn't happen to someone like me, Talia Rhodes. I was the type of person that stuck strictly to facts. If I couldn't see, taste, smell, or touch it, it didn't exist. Now I'm trying hard to cling to my belief system. *"What's really waiting for us on the other side? Where do we go when our time is up? What happens when the clock stops ticking, when we leave this world? When bills become irrelevant and saving for the future ends.*" All of these thoughts are rumbling around in my head as I stare face to face with a woman that is not supposed to be there. She reeks of brimstone. Her eyes are filled with an all-consuming malevolence. She extends her hand towards my head. As she extends it, her form begins to change. I jerk back, a futile effort to prevent her from touching me. I watch in horror as she turns into a grotesque oddity, the likes of which I have never seen. The sheer horror of her appearance is indescribable! She turns into an exact personification of evil. I fight and frantically move my head. I mustn't let her touch me. She looks as if she is enjoying every moment of it. The shadow creatures grab my head and hold it still as my dead ringer's hand gets closer and closer. I feel an intense burning sensation as her fingertips touch the skin on my forehead. Her fingers begin to merge into my flesh, which is something I know there is no known explanation for; the laws of science are being broken as I cry and wince from the intensifying pain forming in my head. My head starts to throb and a loud ringing sound begins to bounce around in my ears. The pain is so intense. It's like having an earache to the tenth power combined with cramps. I feel myself getting weak. My legs are getting heavy. The muscles in my abdomen tighten and throb as well. My posture begins to slump. The pain is unbearable. She merges further and further into me. A dizzying sensation sweeps over me as everything begins to fade.

The sound of birds chirping and rays of sun sneaking in through the slats of the window blinds work collaboratively to awaken me. I try desperately to rustle out of my semi-comatose state. I'm in my living room sprawled out over my couch in a weird unnatural manner. I notice dark red spots smeared in its fabric, as well as on my hands, arms, and torso.

At first, it doesn't really hit me. However, as I continue looking myself over, I begin feeling uneasy. My feet have caked on dirt and remnants of dead leaves stuck to them. "What the…" I sit up. My body feels rigid and my head is throbbing uncontrollably. I manage to stand sloppily to my feet. I look around the room and begin to assess the situation. The room is in complete disarray. The coffee table is broken and lying scattered in pieces across the once pristine carpet and someone or something has made a huge hole in the chocolate colored accent wall. Something definitely isn't right. I try to remember the night before but most of it seems like a dream. It's all pretty much a blur. I can't distinguish the difference between reality and fiction.

Panic begins to set in and my body starts to tremble involuntarily. *"Keep it together."* I think while on the verge of hyperventilating. I tightly wrap my arms around myself as I try to calm down. I desperately want to close my eyes and not accept what I am seeing but a weird compulsion forces me to do exactly the opposite. I continue glossing over the room. My eyes stop at a trail of bloody footsteps leading into the dining room. I lift up one of my feet and check the bottom of it. It's covered in dried dirt and blood. The footsteps appear to be my own. I lower my foot and continue my trek. While walking through the dining room, I look over myself again; this time checking for any cuts or other fresh wounds. I don't find a single scratch. "What have I done?" I mumble as I reluctantly follow the mysterious trail out of the room.

I step into the kitchen, and immediately notice a shovel with pieces of fresh dirt caked on it. I can tell that it's fresh because it still has a clumpy, moist appearance. *"Did I kill someone? And how did I dig through the cold hard pre-winter soil?"* I question mentally as I try to CSI the facts. I walk through the kitchen and head out the back door. I examine the backyard for any freshly dug or covered holes. I'm glad that my backyard has a tall wooden fence that encloses it. The last thing I need is a neighbor to see me covered in blood looking like a deranged killer. I see a small hole near a tree. I proceed over to have a look in it. It's empty. Now I'm confused. *"What did I remove from the hole?"* I rack my brain trying desperately to retrieve any memories of what transpired the night before.

I try to recall the last person with whom I came in contact. *"Kenna,"* quickly illuminates in my mind. In a panicked haste, I run back into the house and scramble around for my phone. I begin removing every couch cushion and metaphorically leaving no stone unturned. I find it of all places, in my back pocket. I swiftly swipe in the pass code and scroll through the recent call list. I tap on the last call log with Kenna's number. Her contact info pops on the screen, accompanied by the sound of ringing. The phone picks up.

"Hello," interrupts the silence.

"Kenna," I respond feeling partially relieved to hear her voice.

"Hey Talia what's up?" She says, while obviously in the middle of something, I can tell by the amount of noise in the background on her end. "So did you have a good night?" She inquires.

"Uh yeah sure," I blurt out, not really giving my full attention to the question.

"You know I miss you," she says warmly.

"Hey let me call you right back okay?" Like a flash of lightening, another person pops in my head, *"Aiden,"* I quickly hang up and scroll until I locate his number. I click on it and it begins to dial. I say hello as soon as the rings stop.

"Hey, I was waiting on you to call me," Aiden says in longing sincere, somewhat angry manner.

"Hi honey," I reply.

"Why didn't you tell about everything that's been going on?"

"I see somebody is happy to hear my voice," I respond sarcastically.

"You don't have to be a smart ass! All I'm saying is that you could've filled me in, I'm sick of finding out things after the fact! Kenna told me everything. I called you like I don't know how many times and it kept going to voicemail!"

"I'm sorry," I reply, which is a rather weak response given the circumstances but I can't think of anything to else to say. Most of my attention is preoccupied with the mystery from the night before. "Hey honey..." I pause, midsentence. In the midst of panic, I clearly forgot to check for one thing, *"Where is Max?"* is the latest addition to the mystery. "Hey Aiden baby, let me call you right back okay?"

"Okay," he responds angrily before abruptly hanging up.

"Max," I yell as I search throughout the house. I check the rest of the rooms on the first floor, no Max. I check the upstairs rooms, still no Max. I make my way to the basement... surprise, no Max. The sound of scratching stops me dead in my tracks. I follow the sound; it leads me to the front door. I open the door and see Max!

ABOUT THE AUTHOR

Anthony D. Phillips was born in Cleveland, Ohio 1980. He lives in Cleveland, Ohio with his wife Tonia and their cats. He is also a father of three and stepfather to two. He is the owner of www.adpbook.com and Dreamer Publishing. Creating stories for others to enjoy, has become an all-consuming passion. He is deeply engrossed in his work as an author. Simply put, he loves what he does.

MORE BOOKS FROM DREAMERPUBLISHING/T.E.G.